Hope

Sarah Branch

Copyright © 2020 Sarah Branch

All rights reserved.

ISBN: 9798604228555

For Lizzie, Katy & Gray.

When the infant had taken it's fill the young mother sat it upright in her lap and looking into the far distance dandled it with gloomy indifference that was almost dislike; then all of a sudden she fell to violently kissing it some dozens of times, as if she could never leave off, the child crying at the vehemence of an onset which strangely combined passionateness with contempt.

- Thomas Hardy, Tess of the D'Urbervilles

CHAPTER ONE

Matthew turns his head to look out the window and sighs. I turn to look out my window and sigh. Charlie, our taxi driver, stares straight ahead at the road and sighs. We've just had a full blown domestic, that is me and Matthew have, Charlie was just an innocent bystander. It was the kind of row that is full of bile, vitriol and jabbed finger accusations. All of our sentences start with "Yeah, but you…". Matthew and I used to laugh behind the backs of those kinds of people; such undignified behaviour. Now we bicker and brawl and not even in a playful, sarcastic way. My husband will undoubtedly say the fight is my fault and he may well be right, but it's so much more fun to disagree with him.

I didn't want to come in the first place and fought against it right up until we walked out the front door. Evidently, by that point I had gotten right on his last nerve. Never one to hold back the way he is feeling when he thinks he is in the right Matthew has spent the whole ten minutes of our journey so far berating me for being such a stubborn cow.

Now there is an awkward silence and I shift uncomfortably in the too tight cocktail dress Matthew insisted I wear, suddenly very aware of my soft doughy tummy straining against the unforgiving crimson polyester. I think it's completely over the top for a house-warming party. I don't care how much of a toff Matthew's old school chum Jonty is, but then I haven't seen the country pile that he inherited from his aunt yet, so perhaps not.

"Stop it!" snarls Matthew without looking at me.

"What?!" I scowl at him, "This dress is really bloody

uncomfortable." He turns to look at me.

"You could probably do with going a couple of sizes bigger these days." he says it earnestly, unaware of the sting in his observation. Charlie gasps and Matthew and I glare at him. The taxi driver shrinks a little in his seat, no doubt feeling our angry eyes fixed on the back of his head.

"I haven't put that much weight on." I say looking down at myself and wondering if I actually believe that. I might be mildly delusional. "Maybe I'm pregnant." I venture. I spot Charlie staring at me in the mirror. Seconds later the car swerves heavily to the left and he mutters an obscenity as he struggles to get it back under control. "Damn it, Charlie." I say.

"Sorry." He seems suitably chastised and shrinks even further into his seat. He will have disappeared altogether soon.

"Did you hear me?" I turn back to Matthew feeling irritated that our taxi driver seems to be paying more attention to me than my own husband. "I said..."

"I heard you" he says and although his head is turned away, I can tell from the tone of his voice he is rolling his eyes at me. "You're not pregnant." There is a rule in our house, that "we" are not officially pregnant until we make it past the twelve-week scan. By that standard, I have never been pregnant. I have, however, had six positive pregnancy tests in the past three years and a whole heap of sadness. This morning, knowing with clinical accuracy that I was precisely three days late, I have convinced myself that I am pregnant, but I knew Matthew would react like this so I was aiming to keep it to myself until I could do a pregnancy test tomorrow morning.

What a contrast this is to the first time we crowded round the positive test. He'd never looked so handsome, the grin spreading across his face as I told him the result. He'd taken my face in his hands and kissed me so tenderly. Then, he had wrapped his arms around me, and I felt safe. I can't remember the last time he hugged me. Have we even touched each other this week? I turn to look at the back of his head as he studiously ignores me in favour of dusky countryside that hurtles past his window. Where once a hint of salt and pepper had licked the edges of his temples, I notice the whole of the back of his head is now a swirling murmuration; flecks of white, silver and grey. I wonder how it is that you can see someone every day and yet barely see them at all.

The car slows and turns into a rough country lane, with high banks on either side. Hedgerows stretch up from the peaks of the banks and block out the fading spring sunshine, making me shiver and pull my pashmina tight around my shoulders. Occasionally a sliver of the setting sun hits my face, warming my skin and blinding me for a second or two. As we bump along the road, I can see a shabby, white bungalow further down on my side of the road. It doesn't seem so grandiose and I wonder if Matthew will feel a bit foolish for having insisted that we dress up so formally. I suspect he feels the same as I notice him fidgeting nervously with his bow tie in the corner of my eye. The taxi continues along the road and to my dismay passes the bungalow and its equally modest neighbour, before turning into a large driveway on the left, packed with Range Rovers, Mercs and BMWs. The house, which might once have been described as a humble hunting lodge by a minor member of the aristocracy, makes my heart sink. It is imposing, grand and utterly beautiful.

Matthew pays Charlie and is skipping up the flight of steps to a tall oak door which curves around at the top in a stately fashion, before I can even fumble my way out of the car. I have to jog, in heels no less, just to reach him before the door is opened by a tall blond woman in a dark shimmering dress. I vaguely recognise her as Jonty's wife, Clemmy. She squeals with delight and grabs my husband in an overly familiar hug. After he's been released from her clutches, she turns to me and offers out a hand.

"Hullo! I'm Clemmy" she says. We have met, at her wedding, but I'm not surprised she's forgotten me. I take her hand, it's limp and damp.

"Tess," I mutter feeling my cheeks redden. She immediately loses interest in me and ushers Matthew into the hallway, huddling against him in a conspiratorial manner. "We have met." I add quietly to myself, before following them in and shutting the door behind me.

"So, where's Bunters then?" my husband always uses Jonty's idiotic nickname from school. I've no idea who came up with Bunters or why, but I did try to look the word up in the Urban Dictionary once and immediately regretted it.

Matthew and Mrs Bunters are oblivious to me hanging back, as they disappear through a door at the end of the hallway in search of the party. Left alone, I stand with my back against the front door. This house is stunning, and I am thankful, if loathe to admit it, that Matthew had insisted on a stuffy, formal dress code. The hallway is wide, with a grand, wide staircase straight ahead, and doors to two rooms on either side. I sneak a peek into the room on the left, where I find mahogany bookcases cover every inch of every wall and groan with what could easily be hundreds of ancient books. I inhale the scent of dusty pages and smile. On the far wall a fireplace dominates, although I'm sad to notice there is no fire in the grate, otherwise I can see myself hiding in this handsome library for the duration of the evening. I suspect no one would even notice if I did. I am tempted but drag myself away and continue down the corridor, following the dim glow of light from the rear of the house and the general din made by overly posh people at social events trying to sound clever and important.

At the end of the corridor is in an immense, modern room which has been bolted on to the back of the house. It is roughly the same height as a standard semi-detached house, like the one Matthew and I live in. To my left is an open plan, sleek kitchen with gleaming white tiles and glossy black worktops. The area is dominated by an island which is roughly the size of my entire kitchen, around which people I don't recognise are stood chatting loudly. The far wall is glass from floor to ceiling and I can just make out the rambling grounds of the house beyond it. Bi-fold doors stretching the width of the room have been pushed open and the guests spill out onto the patio, shivering in their formal wear, many dragging desperately on cigarettes which glow in the twilight like fireflies. To my right, a long table is set for about twenty people. It feels like there are a lot more people here and I am mildly paralysed by a combination of agoraphobia and social anxiety. Before I can turn and run, a man I vaguely recognise as Jonty comes bustling towards me. The ruddy cheeked, jowly countenance and robust waistline spilling over (and under) his tight trouser waistline, is unmistakable. According to Matthew, he has not changed a bit since they were at boarding school together.

"Tess!" he shouts, advancing and grabbing me around the waist to pull me against his pudgy stomach, "Good to see you girl. How are you? Welcome to our humble home!" he says without irony, and I wince half expecting him to slap me hard on the bum. Luckily, he doesn't. In fact, he's so cheerful and friendly, I feel a little bad for resenting being here.

"Thank you. It's very beautiful. I took a quick look at your library. I hope you don't mind. It's absolutely stunning Jonty. I'm really very jealous." He frowns at me and my stomach hiccups with fresh anxiety.

"It's Jobey actually." He clears his throat, "But you should call me Bunters. Everyone does" He makes a heroic effort at joviality, but his smile still falters. I realise he actually looks pretty hurt and my insides churn. Perhaps it was someone else's wedding we had been to, which might explain why his wife didn't recognise me. Curse Matthew for having so many bloody friends and insisting on constantly referring to them by their ludicrous nicknames. I wonder briefly who the hell Jonty is then. To my profound relief and I suspect his, Jobey is quickly commandeered by his willowy wife to take care of some catering arrangements, before the awkward silence can linger.

"Fuck." I mumble and turn away, coming instantly face to face with a small child. Her eyes are wide with the shock and thrill of hearing an adult doing a really naughty swear.

"Mummy!" she yells and turns on her heels, running out onto the patio. I die a little inside and consider actually hiding in the library until the taxi comes back to collect us.

Forced to stand in the centre of the room by myself, without even a drink to distract from the awkwardness, I start to panic in earnest. Matthew spots me from across the room and reluctantly (judging by the scowl on his face) rescues me, hooking his arm through mine and guiding me across the room to a group of his old school friends. They are asking each other what they are driving these days and taking it in turns to waffle on about horsepower, torque and infotainment sytems (is that even a word?). I attempt a look of engaged wonder, but underneath I am wondering if I would get away with faking my own death. I could just drop to the floor, feigning a heart attack and they probably wouldn't even let up their conversation. Just as they are getting stuck into a heated debate on the relative aesthetic merits of the latest Mercedes E-class, Clemmy announces that we are to take our seats, adding with the excitement of a small child about to embark on her first gymkhana, that we have each been allocated a seat.

"Such yay-ness!" I say deadpan and Matthew flings me a venomous look. Everyone huddles around the table, shuffling from seat to seat looking for their name on the intricately decorated place cards. The swirly font is impossibly difficult to read, so the whole process takes far too long, although I am relieved to see Matthew has been seated at the opposite end of the table to me. I suppose this was Clemmy's despicable plan to get everyone mingling and she oversees the horrendously awkward process with an anxious smile on her face. When everyone is finally in their seats, she claps her hands in delight and scurries off to bring out the first course, which she insists that she has been slaving over all day. But, as she hands out the neat little arrangements of chicken liver pate and mini crostini, I'm certain that I have seen these in the Tesco's Finest range. It's hardly the most challenging culinary achievement, to be fair.

The woman to my left groans with delight at every mouthful she shovels in. She is painfully thin, dressed in the kind of sequin clad monstrosity you would expect to see on a drag artist, with approximately five inches of thick make-up, which I am genuinely concerned will undermine the structural integrity of her face. I'm fighting the urge to tell her she appears to have gotten a little face on her make-up. To my relief she engages in hearty conversation with the man on her left, thus negating any need to interact with me. To my right is a bulky man I have never met before.

"Hi," he says chewing on a mouthful of crostini and holds out a hand after wiping it on his trouser leg, "Peter." I shake his chubby hand and introduce myself.

"How do you know Clemmy and...um...Jobey?" I ask out of politeness, not interest. Making small talk takes tremendous effort for me. I loathe it entirely.

"Clemmy is my baby sister." He says and I'm grateful I didn't voice my suspicions about Clemmy's culinary deceit. "You?" he asks, reaching for a bottle of red wine.

"My husband, Matthew, went to school with Jobey." I gesture vaguely to where Matthew is sitting at the other end of the table in between the two hosts. Peter hovers the bottle over my wine glass and I reach out to cover it with my hand.

"Oh no, I'm not drinking, thank you"

"Designated driver, eh? Rotten luck!" he grins revealing a little of the pate mushed into the corner of his crooked teeth, which makes me gag slightly.

"No, we have a taxi." Which I realized was pointless if I wasn't drinking, but Matthew wasn't having any of it. "I'm just not drinking." I smile timidly, hoping this will be an end to it but unfortunately the woman to my left, who had been eyeing up the bottle as it shifted her way, has overhead and she gasps excitedly. I see her glance at my bulging tummy and feel irritated. Even if I am pregnant, I would only be a few weeks. Before I can stop it, a wave of excitement has rippled up and down the table, followed by a cheer. Jobey slaps Matthew hard on the back causing him to splutter out the red wine he had been attempting to drink.

"You never said, you old fox! Congratulations!" Jobey shouts at an utterly perplexed Matthew.

"What are you talking about?" asks Matthew a hesitantly bemused smile hinting at the corners of his mouth.

"The missus being up the duff! You never said." The whole table cheers and I watch my husband's face as any notion of a smile drops and he turns to me. He is furious.

"Tess isn't pregnant." Says Matthew, his glare never leaving my face. I feel myself blushing so hard my cheeks hurt.

"No, just fat I'm afraid!" I say attempting to lighten the mood, but the room is horrifically quiet. Everyone can sense the tension between me and Matthew. I blink furiously to keep back any tears that might humiliate me any further than my husband already has. Eventually there are small murmurs as conversation gradually resumes around me. Peter has turned to talk to the man on his right, but I can tell from his bright pink ears that he too is blushing at the blunder.

As soon as I think everyone has slipped back into their chatter and attention has drifted away from me, I mutter to no-one in particular that I am popping to the loo. In fact, I slip down the corridor and back into the library, gasping in deep breaths to fight back tears. Shivering against the cold air, I curl up in a leather chair where I stay until the taxi comes to collect us several hours later. No one notices I'm gone or comes to find me, and I don't care.

CHAPTER TWO

I wake up the next day, lying on my front and desperate for a wee. Sunshine dapples the bed and I turn onto my back. It releases some of the pressure on my poor tiny bladder, allowing me to lie a little longer, indulging in feline repose. Lazy Sunday mornings have always been my favourite part of the week, like the pause button has been pressed on our hectic lives and I can hide away, having Matthew all to myself. Admittedly, he will often escape my company if he gets the chance, scurrying off to meet with friends or spending hours at the gym. I don't mind though, being perfectly content in my own company. We are poorly suited but perfectly equitable in our differences, although, after last night Matthew might disagree with that. He hasn't said a word to me since I slipped away from the rest of the party. What a miserable evening, for me at least. The taxi ride home wasn't much fun either. His stony silence and palpable anger enough to make Charlie squirm the whole way home.

As I peel away the grogginess of sleep, I am stubbornly refusing to acknowledge the growing urgency in my bladder, and I stroke my swollen midriff (is it really swollen or am I just wishful thinking?). Please let it last this time, I beg silently. It may seem futile, but I refuse to lose hope. There had been no such uncertainty with our first pregnancy. That little blue line signified a certainty, a catalyst into a new world we had both anticipated and embraced eagerly. You just assume, this is parenthood, here we come! That arrogant confidence had been wrenched away from us, along with the first fragile heartbeat. From what we could tell there was never any reason for the miscarriages, which made it all the more cruel and difficult to accept. It was heart-breaking and unfair.

I try not to think about it too much now. Each failed pregnancy feels like a curse. In my twisted logic, the odds of carrying a baby to term dwindles with each new failure, but if I dwell on the babies that didn't make it, I worry that it will somehow put a hex on the baby I'm now convinced that I carry. It's illogical, but desperation can change the way that you think.

Bored of my melancholy thoughts, I pull back the covers and pad across the bedroom to the full-length mirror on our wardrobe door. Turning sideways, I stroke the fabric of my pyjama top flat across my belly and strain to see any evidence of a baby bump. Nothing, but then it would be early days and I am still a little bit fat. Well, perhaps not fat as such. More rotund or chubby if you will. I finally give in to the strain in my bladder and hurry across the hallway towards the bathroom.

Our home is bright and beige and drearily modern. Matthew insists we keep it in showroom condition, no small feat given we both work full time and he adamantly refuses to let me hire a cleaner. I've no idea why. Perhaps he thinks they would riffle through his possessions. Maybe he just wants me to have a miserable life. Who knows? Either way, Saturday mornings have become a ritual of manic cleaning and tidying on my part, with Matthew following behind me to check everything is up to his standard. There's only one room we don't touch. Neither of us can bear to go into the little nursery at the back of the house. All of the flat pack furniture is piled neatly in the corner still in boxes. How stupidly naive we were, rushing out to buy the cot and nursing chair and even the bedding and tiny baby grows, when all we had was a positive pregnancy test and a mountain of misplaced optimism. The door to the ill-fated nursery stays firmly shut, but I always look as I pass, as if I can wish an occupant for the sad little room into existence. Perhaps this time?

In the bathroom, Matthew is standing in front of the sink, digging through the cabinet above it. I sneak through the door, drop my pyjama trousers and ease myself onto the toilet.

His broad shoulders tense angrily, and I wince.

"Damn it, Tess..." he says through gritted teeth as I gush noisily into the toilet. I feel it coming but tense too late as a dainty toot echoes from the bowl. Matthew stops what he is doing and grips the edge of the sink, his knuckles whitening as his temper grows. I wonder when exactly he lost his sense of humour. Attempting to dissipate the tense atmosphere, I smile up at him, but he keeps his back turned on me. I watch as he takes a deep breath and reaches back into the cupboard. He brushes aside a bottle of clench inducingly expensive aftershave that I bought him for his last birthday, which had always been his favourite. Just before Christmas, a new bottle of a different brand of aftershave had appeared, its obnoxious scent enough to make my eyes water at ten paces. There was never any explanation as to where it had come from. I do wonder where it came from. It is this new bottle he now places in his wash bag, which is perched on the edge of the sink.

"Are we going somewhere?" I ask through a lazy yawn.

"I am" he replies.

"Another business trip? Surely the packing can wait until later. I was thinking we could head into town this afternoon and have a mooch around the Farmer's Market, maybe get something nice for dinner?" I am rambling in the hope his mood will lighten, but if anything it just seems to make things worse. He is completely ignoring me, fastidiously focused on his task. When he finishes, he turns to look at me. His expression is the kind that is normally reserved for traffic wardens and left-wing politicians; pure unabridged resentment.

"I'm leaving you." he says after a dramatic pause. I understand the words, but somehow can't comprehend what he is saying. I sit semi-naked, still perched on the toilet, hair dishevelled, and my face crumpled from sleep. He walks out of the bathroom as I desperately fumble to make myself decent, before stumbling after him. In the bedroom he stands by the wardrobe, flipping casually through the hangers as if browsing through the racks at Next. He pauses occasionally to select and review an item before folding it carefully and placing it into the brown leather holdall his mother bought him for Christmas, which sits open at his feet. My heart is hammering so hard in my chest it hurts. I feel sick.

"Where are you going?" my voice is barely a whisper across the quiet room. He lets the question hang as he continues to pack. Although I know he's not thinking about his answer. He's just enjoying leaving me hanging for a response. My stomach lurches dramatically as it dawns on me that this is really happening. My husband is actually leaving me. What the hell did I do?

"I'm going to stay with a friend," he finally speaks, casually as if discussing dinner plans, "until I can find something more permanent."

"But...why?" my voice pitches hysterically. He stops packing and turns to me with a pitiful frown. I hate being patronised at the best of times, but I'm struggling to muster any anger towards him. There's nothing but shock and fear.

"C'mon Tess. This..." he flips his hand back and forth between us, the gap never felt so big, "it hasn't been working for a long time now."

"No..."

"I think if you are really honest with yourself, you would be able to admit that our marriage has been over for a long time." He turns and continues packing.

"No. I still love you...I love you so much." My voice trails off. "Matthew...please..."

"Don't do this Tess," his anger is rising again, "Don't try to emotionally blackmail me into staying. It's not fair." I open my mouth to reply but can't find the words. After ten years of marriage, I wonder for the first time if I might actually be a little scared of him. His hunched broad shoulders cast an intimidating shape of a man I thought I knew so intimately, and now feels like a complete stranger. I stand dumb and watch as Matthew zips up his holdall, preparing to leave. As he turns to walk out of the room, I hold up my hands and stand between him and the door. This is my last chance to keep him here. He frowns dangerously, furrowing his eyes into shadow.

"I just..." I stop and take a deep breath to calm myself, "I don't understand. You can't just walk out and not talk this through with me." My voice grows surer as I speak.

This is my husband, not the angry stranger he seems to have turned into. But as I watch him, it seems to me something significant has changed in him.

"Get out of the way Tess." He says through clenched teeth.

"No." I stand a little straighter, trying to look brave even though I don't feel it, "We are going to talk this through."

"Get out of the way." His voice is a warning growl, but in my desperation, I continue to push my luck. It briefly occurs to me that I'm not at all desperate for him to stay, but somehow, because the choice has been taken from me, I feel galvanised to do anything to stop him from leaving.

"Please give us a chance to work this through. Matthew, please." He rushes at me then, barging past he pushes me hard backwards. I stumble and land hard on my arse. Standing over me, his cheeks red with anger, he runs a shaky hand through his slick black hair and points at me.

"Just stop. I'm leaving." he practically screams the words at me and for the first time I am really scared. Then he leaves. I sit shocked and winded on the floor listening to his hasty footsteps as he charges out of the house.

Several hours later, I lie once more upon the bed, the sheets and pillows around me drenched with tears. The sunlight has long since faded into a bleak grey rainstorm, which thrashes waves of raindrops against the windows. The room has become cold and dark and I shiver, refusing to pull the warm duvet around me. Through all of the shock and despair, however, is an unwelcome recognition that I had somehow known this was coming. My inability to give him a child seems to have been my biggest sin, but social awkwardness may have come a close second. It all seems too trivial; surely my love for him would be strong enough to overlook a million flaws all more substantial and yet I cannot forgive myself for my own defects that have eroded his love for me. I have failed us both.

The events of the weekend swirl around me like an angry crowd, roaring angry recriminations until my head is thumping and I need to peel myself off the bed. Feeling hoarse and dehydrated, I make my way shakily down to the kitchen to pour myself a glass of water. While it soothes my throat, nothing can pacify the wretched feeling in my chest. Draining the remaining water in my glass, I spend a few minutes rummaging in the cupboard under the sink finally producing a cheap bottle of bargain plonk coated in dust, which I had been banned from consuming on the grounds of it being "a bit common". It had been a jokey gift from an old friend; a reminder our student days when we had mixed together the cheapest alcohol we could lay our hands on into toxic punch, topped up with cheap wine. But it had been swiftly confiscated by Matthew for the sake of propriety and condemned to the back of the cupboard until it could be put to good use as a donation to the village summer fete or taken to the dinner party of someone we really hated. I sloppily pour a glass and take a large glug, which burns my tender throat.

With the glass in one hand and the bottle in the other, I slink through to the living room and sling both down on the fine mahogany sideboard that Matthew inherited from his wealthy grandparents, with scant regard for its delicate and ancient patina. Matthew would have had a complete shit-fit if he'd seen my irreverence towards his beloved heirloom. I giggle to myself as I jab at the on button of a small hi-fi on the edge of the sideboard. Beside it are Matthew's collection of high-brow classical compilations and a couple of rock bands from the Seventies, which I childishly push off the edge. In the drawer below it I find my music collection, deemed unsuitable to be on public show, from which I dig out a couple of CDs.

The music blasts but I turn it up louder. Rubbing my eyes precipitates a few rogue tears to spill out down my raw cheeks. Still in my pyjamas, I grab my glass and the bottle beside it and crawl into Matthew's armchair and rest my cheek on its withered arm. For hours I sit, nursing the wine, staring blankly across the room, occasionally singing in quiet raspy tones but more often in loud tuneless ones. As the wine bottle empties the dull ache in my chest subsides ever so slightly and my dismay drifts. I start to tell myself that it is a good thing that Matthew is gone. We were just too different in the end. Accepting this, brings little comfort and is, in itself a fresh heartbreak. In fact, it feels like I'm betraying Matthew, even though he is gone and doesn't care. It's one thing to accept that a ten-year relationship is over. It's another thing altogether to accept that the last decade of my life has been a pretence; a charade of happiness. I slip into restless mourning for how my life could have turned out.

For several days I embrace the purgatory, swinging from juvenile indulgence to utter misery. Having called in sick at work (in fairness I have been nauseous every morning, but hangovers are seldom considered an illness per se), I struggle to adjust to my new Matthew-free life. This has, to some extent, involved seeking out my estranged husband's most prized possessions, which had been abandoned in his haste to leave me, and destroying them. His vintage vinyl record collection proved rather more resilient than I had anticipated, but easily succumbed to his Titanium golf driver, when balanced between a George II Walnut card table and a rather gaudy bronze of a half-naked lady, which I hoped was hideously expensive. I particularly enjoy the moment when the driver misses and bounces off the table taking a wedge out of the elderly veneer. By the time I have finished, all of his cosseted golf clubs are decidedly L shaped, which makes me laugh like a lunatic.

It is all fun and games until day two, when I wake at midday and groggily open the curtains to find a 'For Sale' sign had been deposited in my beautifully chaotic wildflower bed. I stand dumbfounded at this fresh assault. The finality of this gesture pushes me to dispense the Lambrini a little earlier in the day than has become routine, having re-stocked on the innocuous bargain booze via my online weekly shop, which is now more liquid than solid. By three pm, my senses dulled, and inhibitions drowned, I reach for my mobile to call him for the first time since he left me. One hour later my calls flip straight to voicemail and by seven they are being blocked altogether. I slip into a fitful sleep curled up on his chair, my mobile lying smashed on the floor.

When I wake the room is cold and dark. I sit up gingerly and rake my fingers through my greasy, matted hair. My back spasms as I stand and attempt to stretch away the aches. Suddenly, a thought hits me like a truck. A fresh wave of nausea rises up in my throat and I clasp a shaking hand to my mouth. The vomit is already burning the back of my throat when I kneel before the toilet and empty my guts. When the sickness has finally subsided, gripping the toilet unsteadily, I pull myself up and reach into the bathroom cabinet which has been gaping open since Matthew's departure.

Precisely ten minutes later I look at the small white stick. The blue line confirms it. I'm pregnant.

CHAPTER THREE

The next morning, I drag myself into the office, despite the brutal queasiness, which could have been either a hangover or morning sickness; I can no longer tell although I haven't touched a drop of alcohol since the test and I am racked with guilt at the damage I could have done. I have worked at Johnson Logistics Ltd since graduating eleven years ago and have failed, so far, to truly grasp what it is this company actually does. The only thing I can be sure of is that no one seems to notice, and I really don't care. I stagger up to the second floor where Operations and Finance are situated, in a smart but clinical open plan office that stretches from one end of the building to the other. Sales and senior management (including my estranged husband) take up the third floor, which is subdivided neatly into executive offices. Everyone else is stuck on the ground floor, which overlooks a rather grim, grey car park. Here it is the kind of corporate environment where everyone knows everyone-else and everyone else's business too, so I try to avoid eye contact as I weave in amongst the desks to get to mine.

Obscuring a coveted spot by the window, my desk is clear and tidy, with only a picture of me and Matthew on our wedding day, in small frame tucked away by the side of the computer monitor. I can't bear to look at it and turn the picture face down, before rushing to the Ladies to violently eject the scarce contents of my stomach for the second time today. By the time I arrive back at my desk, the lithe figure of Suzy Collins is perched elegantly on the edge, her customary skin-tight pencil skirt clinging to a pair of perfectly contoured thighs. Suzy has killer legs and a ridiculously taut bottom and judging by her wardrobe, she wants everyone to know it. I feel the bile rise again as I approach and realise that the picture from my desk is in her hand. I approach the irritatingly perky twenty-something year old and snatch it out of her hands. It should be illegal to be so young and attractive.

"Oh!" she yelps, and then smiles disarmingly at me, "Hey hun. Aww look at you…" She slurs and I bristle. I am of the opinion that anyone who calls people "hun" should be pushed off a cliff. Suzy works up in Sales and had been transferred onto Matthew's team back in November. He spoke of her often, calling her a "bright young thing" with "stacks of ambition", confirming to me that she is in fact, a massively irritating bitch. I have only spoken with her once before and I despise her. Before I can respond to her despicably cheerful greeting, she spreads her arms to take me hostage in an awkward hug. Despite my head being wedged against her shoulder, for she is considerably taller than my dumpy frame, I see several members of the Finance department observing the strange encounter, looking up from their desks to frown. Generally speaking, human interaction before the first cup of coffee has been ingested and assimilated, is considered both rude and unnecessary. Physical interaction is nothing short of an abomination.

"Hi" I say as I manage to escape the unwelcome embrace.

"I heard you hadn't been well, how you doing now? You look a bit peaky hun." she says giving me a pouty, mock grimace. I wonder briefly how she knows or why she cares that I have been unwell, but mostly I just want her to piss the hell off and leave me alone. Besides the fact I have a week's worth of work to catch up on, I haven't had my morning coffee and I'm not even sure if I will be able to stomach it, which is making me even more irritable.

"I'm fine now, actually." I say curtly, settling into my chair and switching on my pc.

"Are you sure, hun? Cos you look rough as. Do you know what I mean?" I'm glaring at her but she beams back enthusiastically and pats my arm tentatively in a gesture which suggests that she is more concerned about breaking a nail than comforting me, "Matthew has been so worried about you." My stomach lurches. What has Matthew been saying to her? Does she know we are separated? Why has he been speaking to Suzy of all people about how he is feeling, when all my attempts to contact him are met with a brick wall. Suzy smiles at me then, in a way that is so devoid of warmth, her malice is palpable. She knows her blow has hit its mark.

"Oh, by the way, this is my expenses claim, would you mind hun?" she flings the paper across the desk to me and turns on her heel, sweeping through the office before I've had the chance to even register my own shock. I take a shaky breath and close my eyes. For a moment the room is spinning and the sick feeling that has never quite gone away is rushing up through my gullet. It takes several moments to overcome the impulse to both cry and vomit. When my head has cleared a little, I pick up Suzy's expense claim form, crumpling it slowly into a ball and dropping it into my bin, while scowling at her departing form. Who does that bitch think she is? I'm a Senior Finance Manager. I don't do expenses. I turn back to my computer to check the progress of my ancient pc, which is still struggling to wake up (I know how it feels). After a few guilty moments, I pull the crumpled sheet out of the bin and weave my way through the desks to the Payroll processing team, where I hand the form over. Beryl, by far the oldest person in the company (and possibly also in the country), looks up at me with a kind and maternal smile followed by a frown.

"Christ love," she says, "you look like shit!"

"I feel it Beryl" I say attempting a weak smile. "You ok?"

"Same old, same old" she responds absently, scanning through the claim form and turning back to her computer. It's still too early for human interaction in the Finance department of Johnson Logistics. Back at my desk, when I am finally able to login, I realise with dismay that I have over one hundred unread emails, none of which look either urgent or interesting; except one. My line manager, Tanya sent me an email three days ago requesting an "urgent chat". She has only been with the company since October last year, when she and I both applied for the same job as Finance Director. I assume from her attitude and the fact that she has been steadily piling the pressure on me, that she expects me to be jealous of her success. Perhaps she feels threatened by me, although I have never been the type for backstabbing. My failure to win the promotion had left me feeling gutted, but I had accepted the decision with relative equanimity and aplomb, earnestly attempting to form productive and harmonious relationship with my new boss. Even though, if I'm entirely honest, underneath I've been seething with jealous rage, I am trying to be the bigger woman. I've mentally given her the affectionate nickname Cowface McGee, but I'm really not bitter.

I look up to see if she is in her little room at the far end of the office while mumbling an obscenity under my breath. The light appears to be off, so I assume I am off the hook for the time being. But then, as if summoned from the depths of hell, the door swings open and she strides in. She is a formidable sight, clad in full bike leathers with a bright pink motorcycle helmet grasped in her delicately manicured hand. Sweeping her gaze across the room, she finally fixes her stare on me, points a chubby finger and then curls it up to summon me towards her. I rise reluctantly from my desk as she turns and marches into her office. By the time I have followed her in, she is sat at her desk, unforgiving leather trousers pinching in at her rotund waist in a way that suggests her internal organs are being mashed in an unnatural manner. Having discarded her leather jacket onto the back of her chair, I can see she is wearing a beige see through blouse, putting both her lacy black bra and mountainous bosom on full show. I try not to stare as I sit in the chair on the opposite side of her desk and wait. She slips a pair of glasses onto the end of her nose and it makes her look even older than her fifty-odd years (I guess) and taps a dayglo pink nail against the keyboard. The tip-tap noise sets my teeth on edge.

She continues to ignore me for several deliberately unnerving minutes, before taking her glasses back off and turning to face me.

"So," she places both hands flat on the desk in front of her, "how are we feeling?" I presume by "we" she means me.

"Much better now, thank you." I try to seem to a little worse for wear to keep up the charade, although according to

Beryl there was really no need. In my decade with the company I have only had a dozen or so days off sick, many of which had been due to miscarriages, and Cowface McGee is perfectly aware of this.

"Good," she says in a curt manner that implies she actually couldn't care less. "I hear that you and Matthew have separated. I'm sorry to hear that Tess." For a moment I am, yet again gob smacked. Was it now common knowledge that my marriage had fallen apart? Did these people have nothing better to talk about? Why am I even surprised, when this is par for the course in this toxic, corporate hell-hole. This time, rage, not bile is swelling in my throat and all I can do is nod, silently seething. "How do you think the two of you will get on working for the same company, in the same office no less?"

"I... well... I hadn't actually thought about it too much." I say.

"Just speaking as a friend," she says, knowing full well she is nothing of the sort, "do you not think it might be a bit awkward for you both?" I study her face for clues as to where she is headed with her line of questioning, but her poker face game is good.

"I think we are both adults and can handle ourselves in an adequately professional manner." As long as he doesn't speak to me, or look at me or in fact, breathe in my presence. That is, until I've calmed down enough to show him what he's missing. And when he realises that I'm pregnant, and this time I'm not going to lose the baby, he'll be begging me to take him back. I just hope the house doesn't sell in the meantime.

"Okay," she says, "well here's the rub. I've been asked to cut some heads, well one position at least. I'm thinking this might be an opportunity to get a fresh start." I sit up startled. I hadn't expected this.

"Sorry, you're making me redundant?" I ask.

"No, I'm offering you first dibs at voluntary redundancy" she says impatiently, "You could get away from all of the awkwardness that I'm sure will follow. Trust me Tess, I've been through two divorces now and I don't care how grown up or professional you think you are it always ends up bitter and messy." I shudder at the D word, we're a long way off that, "This could be a great opportunity for you. You can find a new job, push your career forward. Or even take a bit of time off with the redundancy money." I sit quietly thinking about what she is saying, seeing the sense at her suggestion, but not sure whether to trust her. I don't love my job but right now some stability and continuity would be a comfort. I know that I can support myself and the baby when the time comes. Tanya sees me hesitate.

"Honestly Tess, you don't think you will find it difficult seeing him with *her* every day?" Tanya stares at me unblinking and ambivalent. I have one of those moments where you feel your stomach drop, like you are in an elevator that has plunged twenty floors.

"With who?" I ask in a small voice.

"Oh dear," she attempts a little humility, "you didn't know?"

"Know what?" my voice rises and quivers a little. I'm not sure I want to know the answer to my question.

"Well, I'm sorry to be the one to tell you this," she doesn't look sorry at all, she looks like a predator going in for the kill, "Matthew and Suzy...it's been going on for a while. I'm sorry, I thought you knew." The room is swimming and I sit dead still willing it to stop. The brass neck of that woman, coming into my office and hugging me. Now it occurs to me that everyone knows about them, those looks this morning when she hugged me. Everyone knows but me.

I'm generally a pretty calm person, and certainly not a violent one, but at that moment a searing hot anger consumes every cell in my body. I storm out of the office, taking two steps at a time up to the third floor, and barge my way into Matthew's office. There I find Suzy perched on the edge of Matthew's desk, leaning over his computer, practically rubbing her boobs in his face. I make a guttural noise that could have come from a wild animal and the pair stop mid laugh to stare at me.

"Jesus, Tess...you look like shit." Matthew says with a smirk. Quickly sensing my anger, Suzy's smile drops, and she starts to back away, but my rage is focused entirely on him. He swiftly ushers Suzy out, closing the door behind her and clasps his hands on my upper arms. My heart is thudding so hard in my chest that I can barely breathe.

"How could you?" I growl at him.

"What? How could I what?" he looks genuinely confused. He is so convinced his lies will work with me.

"With her!" I spit at him, jabbing a finger towards the closed the door. His face waivers and colours slightly, caught out at last.

"Listen Tess," he grips me more strongly, "you and I... it's been over for a while... we just couldn't admit it to ourselves, could we? And besides, Suzy is just a fling. It's nothing serious." I push him away. It takes all the strength in my anger.

"How long has it been going on?" I shout. He shrugs. "How long?" I screech.

"Oh, for God's sake! I don't know. About six months maybe? Does it matter?" At that point I see red. I barely register as I pick up the closest thing to hand, it may have been a stapler or a hole-punch and I hurl it straight at his head. Disappointingly he manages to dodge it and it bounces off the wall, so I continue slinging whatever I can get my hands on in his general direction, which is tricky in his slick minimalist office. It's not long until I'm grappling with a large potted yucca plant in the corner, which I struggle to lift and eventually have to abandon. I feel tears streaming down my face as I scream obscenities at him, both of us circling his desk as he attempts to evade the missiles that I throw at him. Eventually, site security arrive, one of them clasping me tight around the middle, until I'm calm enough to be removed. Matthew at this point has escaped to a safe distance and as I am manhandled away, I see him stood with Suzy as she gently comforts him, a tender hand stroking down his face where I fervently hope I have managed to make a successful strike.

I am escorted back down to my floor where Tanya ushers me into her office.

"I think I'm ready to consider your offer." I gasp, still out of breath from my exertions, whilst struggling to pull my clothes back into order. She assesses me; I am a shambles.

"Now Tess, you are an intelligent woman. Precisely why on earth would I pay you fourteen grand in redundancy, when you've given me the perfect opportunity to fire you for gross misconduct?" her look is severe with an undertone of smugness. I'm crestfallen. "I take it you are not going to deny that you just physically assaulted another member of staff? There are many witnesses who are claiming that you have." I'm staring at the floor barely able to process what has just happened. In the end I just nod dumbly and rise from the seat. I turn to leave the office before Tanya can say another word. If I'm being fired for physically assaulting someone, I might be tempted to have a pop at her too. In for a penny and all that. But I am all out of fight.

The security guards, who have been standing sentry outside the office, walk me to my desk. With what little dignity I can muster, I clear my desk of what meagre personal possessions there are, grab my handbag and allow myself to be escorted off site. I leave the wedding picture face down on my desk.

CHAPTER FOUR

Everyone has somewhere they go to when they need to feel safe. For me, it has always been my Dad's house. He seems somewhat incongruous in the elegant three-storey townhouse; there is only one occasion I can remember him wearing anything smarter than tatty old jeans and his big holey jumpers that smell unmistakably of Dad, and that was my wedding day. Back in the eighties he and my Mum made a small fortune syndicating a game show format they had devised and produced in the UK. Requiring normal members of the public to make absolute arses of themselves on assault courses for the schadenfreude of tv audiences was a formula that proved much more successful across Eastern Europe and Japan, but still managed to become well known in the UK. This earned me my nickname of "Bounce-time Girl" at school; nobody needs that, least of all a chubby teenage girl. Having found himself suitably well off enough to send his only daughter to private school, my father did just that. Unfortunately. Once the other pupils found out about my parent's endeavours the nickname stuck and I was forever singled out as the nouveau riche girl who didn't belong amongst the offspring of Lords, minor members of the aristocracy and multi-millionaire business tycoons.

Despite their success, my father remained unapologetically and unmistakably working class, to the distress of their upper-middle class neighbours and my upper-class school mates. The house they bought on the edge of the grounds of Winchester Cathedral would, in anyone else's hands have been considered a pretentious show of wealth and success. For my parents, it was just a beautiful old house with huge sash windows bringing in the natural light they loved. I recall it seeming enormous to me as a child, but always homely and safe, despite the absence of my Mother who had died when I was two weeks old.

They told me she had been driving to my Aunt Sophie's for a cup of tea and a general break from her newborn daughter. Dad had been sleeping on the couch with me cuddled up on his chest after a particularly rough sleepless night, when the policeman had knocked at the door. They said it had been a tragic car accident, as they so often were in those days before compulsory seatbelts, when cars were precarious metal monsters that crumbled at the slightest impact. I hadn't really missed her as such; it's hard to miss what you've never had. She was a constant shadow in the periphery of my childhood, and I remember feeling a morbid curiosity as I closely watched my friends with their mothers. I suspect they thought I was a very odd little girl as a result.

As I got older I was given the run of the house and found it easy to get lost in the vast high-ceilinged rooms. My bedroom, at the front of the house, had a large window seat, where I would sit for hours and watch crowds swarm in and out of the cathedral grounds. Since my self-imposed exile, this is pretty much all I have done. It's busy today and amongst the throb of endless tourists and scruffy students milling about, I seek out someone different who can hold my attention a little better. I restlessly scan the crowds, curled up as best I can with my cumbersome bump, a fleece blanket wrapped around me despite the dwindling autumn sun.

Just as I can feel the old ruminations of Matthew and the baby and what is next for me intruding my thoughts, I spot her. I cannot at first fathom why she has caught my eye, although she is very pretty without a doubt, she seems at first glance rather plain. She strides along the path towards the cathedral, long, lightly tanned legs with ballet slippers beating steps that look almost like she is about to break into a dance; something elegantly energetic like a Samba. She throws a look over her shoulder and I can see she is grinning back at someone. Pulling her long brown hair over her shoulder, she turns to face a man that is running up behind her.

Hope

He seems to be a blur at first, catching her as she continues her stride but walking backwards now. He slips a strong arm around her waist and lifts her up. Laughing, she wraps her slender legs around his waist and her arms eagerly around his neck. He stops walking, right in the middle of the pavement, and they kiss.

I watch the nauseating scene, as annoyed tourists stream around them. They are completely lost in one another. She pulls away from the kiss and nudges his nose with hers, wriggling free from his embrace. Looping a lazy arm around his waist, she leans into his armpit (she is at least a head height shorter than him) and they take a more casual pace, moving past the cathedral itself and into the grounds that lay beyond. I'm both irritated by and envious of this woman. What did she do to be worthy of such an open display of tenderness? I try to recall the most affectionate public gesture Matthew had ever given and can only recall a handful of attempts by me, met with a grimace and rebuttal. He would ask what I thought I was doing before withdrawing. I stopped trying after a while. Perhaps I was doing it wrong.

A gaggle of young mother's flock into the edge of the grounds, laying out a large picnic blanket amongst the crooked ancient gravestones on the perimeter under the sparse cover of the ancient oaks that cluster around the old building. I count five incredibly thin, perfectly coiffured and manicured young woman, but oddly just four babies, imprisoned in their luxury Bugaboo and Silver Cross pushchairs. I watch on as they chatter and smile, unloading Tupperware containers brimming with sticks of carrot and cucumber and depositing crawling, toddling children onto the floor. The women seem utterly focused on their conversations; they barely seem to notice the babies.

As I watch with growing unease, one little renegade in a non-gender specific sunshine yellow romper suit makes a break for it. Within seconds rebel baby is off the sacred picnic blanket and steaming towards the path. I look back at the mums, but nobody has noticed. Panic is rising in my chest and I slip one leg off the window seat, as if I am going to run out of the house in my jim-jams and save some stranger's baby from being crushed underfoot by an impending hoard of

Japanese tourists (they rarely travel in groups of less than thirty I've noticed). As I watch, the baby stops dead, looking down at his/her chubby fist. Rebel baby rocks slightly and then raises his/her hand. I squint and can just about make out the writhing shape of worm pincered in the baby's clumsy fingers as it rises up to his/her mouth. Suddenly, one of the mums swoops down and lifts the baby onto her hip. It howls with the injustice of losing its quarry which has tumbled to the ground. I can't help but smile. It's been a while and it feels like my skin might fracture under the unfamiliar upward curve of my lips. I sigh, settling back onto the window seat and resting my forehead against the glass again.

I feel a fleeting urge to stroke my tummy, which is now tediously rotund. I have been waiting in vain for six long months to miscarry. It seems impossible to me that a tiny human is growing, bunched up under my skin. Even when I started to feel the first tentative flutters of movement, I struggled to believe that I was going to have a baby. I'm no more prepared for motherhood now. My existence barely exists beyond this damp window sill where I wallow in self-pity and despise myself all the more for it. With the house now sold, I could be doing as Tanya suggested and start preparing for a fresh start, but I can't. I just can't.

By early afternoon, the steady stream of people passing through my view has started to ebb. The gaggle of mum's has long since departed, frustrated by the impertinence of their offspring who repeatedly insisted upon being entertained, fed and changed thus inhibiting their mother's incessant gabbling. A small group of sullen teenagers sit in silence, disregarding one another to squint at their mobiles. Two elderly ladies promenade, with more elegance and ceremony than their location requires, up to the cathedral entrance. I can just about make them out as they scowl at the prices on the entrance notice board before promenading away indignantly.

At the end corner of the graveyard, a solemn faced student sits cross legged on the grass nursing a tatty paperback. She stands out to me, as both part of the scene and distinctly disconnected from it at the same time, as she looks up from the book from time to time to see what is going on around her. After watching her for some time, I realise she has not turned a single page of the novel clutched in her hand; it's a front. Despite the rare October sunshine she is wearing a thick black leather jacket, and her long black hair is twisted up into a messy bun. Not the trendy kind though. She looks a state.

Just as I start to feel a sense of calm, indicating that my vigil has achieved its aim of distraction, my heart jolts. Two women are walking out of the cathedral entrance, arm in arm. One is middle aged, the other I guess is in her late twenties, but they look so strikingly similar they must be mother and daughter. As they walk the younger woman absently strokes her extended belly. It is as full and round as mine, at that stage of pregnancy where approximately eighty-five per cent of the male population would feel comfortable asking a woman when she is due, without too much fear of being beaten liberally by a sobbing fat lady (and quite right too).

The two women walk at a casual pace, talking and smiling, lost in the comfort of each other's company. I would give anything to have my mother with me right now or even just to have a comforting memory to turn to. She is all but a stranger to me, but I cling to the image of a woman who would have been warm and loving. She could have been an intolerable bitch for all I know, but since childhood I have had to fill in the missing details of this ghost of a woman, using only other people's vague memories and my own imagination. Elaborately biased to fulfil whatever my need had been at the time, thinking of the mother she could have been has always left me feeling sad and angry.

Right now, my ghost mother is calm and comforting. She tells me I'm strong enough to get through this and I'm better off without him. But this doesn't make me feel any better. It's hideously unfair that I have been robbed of the one person who could have helped me through all of this. All calmness vanishes in an instant, I'm gripped with jealousy and bitterness. I don't want to see anymore happy people enjoying their normal, tragedy-free lives, so I gather my blanket around me and leave the room.

Downstairs, my father is sat at the kitchen table, his

mobile pinned to the side of his head. Although he is not speaking I can see from the redness of his cheeks and the whiteness of his knuckles as he grips the phone in his hand, he is furious. I pull out a chair, lifting it gently so the heavy wooden legs don't scratch against the tiled floor. He doesn't look at me. We sit in silence, the distant murmur of the voice on the other end of the line rumbles on monotonously into my father's ear. I sit in the path of sunlight which is streaming through the window, feeling it warm my skin until finally, without a word, he hangs up and brings his fist down hard on the table making me jump.

"What the..." I say.

"If I ever see that little shit ever again," he spits through clenched teeth pointing his finger at me, "I will kill him." His face has turned bright scarlet and I can only sit in shock staring at him. "He's gone too far this time. I swear to God..."

"Sorry Dad. What? Who? I don't know what's going on..." although I sense I know what this might be about.

"Matthew..."

"Oh. Was that him?" I ask trying and failing not to sound too eager. Even after everything that has happened, I still get butterflies in my stomach at the mention of his name

"No. It was his bastard solicitor." I wince. Now I am caught off guard. I'd hoped it might be Matthew asking about how I was doing, checking I was coping ok. His radio silence is deafening and cruel.

"The divorce lawyer? That sounds ominous." Dad seems to shrink down in his chair for a moment. He sighs angrily. Matthew started divorce proceedings almost immediately after I had retreated from our house to my father's home. Given my state of mind and physical condition, we had agreed that my Dad would handle the situation and deal with solicitors for me, with the brief that it should be as quick and painless as possible. Matthew's solicitor had stressed there was no possibility of reconciliation and it would be better for all involved to just get the deed done. We were all in agreement. My marriage was over.

"Matthew wants half of the investment portfolio in the divorce settlement."

"What? But most of that came from Mum's life insurance money! He's already had half of the money from the house and he probably put less than a couple of thousand into our investments." I say miserably. Though I would normally be inclined to put up one hell of a fight, I'm just too tired and sad to take him on.

"He's not having a penny. After what he's done to you..." Dad is turning a peculiar shade of purple. It was bad enough that Matthew had left me for another woman. The fact he had cited the grounds for divorce being my unreasonable behaviour towards him (i.e. that one violent incident at work) had sent Dad into an apoplectic rage he had never quite recovered from. My ex, it seems, is a bit of a turd.

"Dad, calm down." I reach across the table to take his hand in mine.

"I will not calm down. Who does that little prick think he is?"

"Dad...deep breaths...honestly, after everything that has happened, I don't know why you're even surprised. I'm not." My voice is quivering, but I refuse to cry. My Dad looks at me then, the colour of his cheeks slowly returning to a more natural hue, but his eyes are full of sadness. "You know what? Fuck it. Let him have it" I add meekly.

"No!" my father explodes again, "What the hell Tess?! That little shit isn't getting another single penny out of you, or me for that matter..." I sit quietly as my father's rage spills out of him. The lecture goes on for some time as I'm urged to pull myself out of it and fight for what's mine, but I'm all out of fight. He tries one last tack as his anger simmers down to a low-lying vehemence. "It would be different if you told him about the baby."

"It would," I shrug, "but then he would want to be involved. I'd have to let him back into my life and I think I've only just gotten to the point where I can close the door on him for good." Looking up I take in my father's frown and lean across the table to put my hand on his again. "Dad, I need to move on. I need to move away from him and I need this divorce to be over quickly." My father looks heartbroken. I think for a moment, his eyes might be welling up but I look away as he composes himself and when I look back his eyes are dry.

"Tess, I really think..." I hold up a hand to stop him.

"I have enough money to get by. I just need to move on Dad." He looks at me for a long time. He is breathing hard and I can tell he is struggling, wishing my Mum was here to back him up, and not for the first time. Finally, he takes a deep breath, looks down at the table, and puts his hand on top of mine sandwiching it between his.

"Ok." he says quietly and then he gets up and stalks out of the room in a manner that suggests he is mentally planning a suitably painful death for my soon to be ex-husband.

CHAPTER FIVE

As I lie in bed I consider, not for the first time, that I have made some appalling life choices. When I came to view this house, on an unseasonably warm autumn day, I was captivated by its cottage charm, with daydreams of cosy winter evenings by the fire in the snug little lounge at the front of the house. It was a considerable downgrade from the home I had shared with Matthew, but perhaps that was the point of this quaint two up two down, Victorian terrace. For the first time since he had left me, I was taking control and making my life what I wanted it to be. Buoyed by this new focus, I had fallen for the first house I had seen and made a snap decision on the spot. This was my bolthole, my new sanctuary. Tucked away on a side street from the obscure little market town, I was a safe distance from Matthew, who I have since found out from stalking him online, has moved into Suzy's rented flat in Guildford. My house is smack bang in between Guildford and Winchester, which is just over thirty minutes away. Close enough to feel the support of my father if I need it, but not too close to feel tempted to rely heavily on him. I feel like I've found the place I want to be.

  Tonight though, on review, my decision making may have been flawed. As I nurse a bursting bladder and consider, quaint cottages are all very nice, until you are heavily pregnant, bursting for the loo and the only toilet is down a rickety set of stairs. By the time I have this epiphany I am days away from my due date, with a bump large enough to prevent me from seeing my feet as I attempt to negotiate the narrow wooden steps, which are littered with boxes and books that haven't found a home for yet, hinting at my subconscious suicidal tendencies. Between the soreness in the small of my back, exhaustion from lack of sleep and the general grumpiness that accompanies most women into their third trimester, I've had enough. When I finally heft myself onto the toilet and gush like a prize-winning racehorse, I am mentally planning to move out. Unfortunately, I have, in what I thought was an extremely savvy move, elected to pay a full year of rent up front, thinking it would help me budget my dwindling funds. Just eleven months left, I think to myself as I shiver against the cold, which seems to seep through the thick walls.

Standing up to wash my hands, I catch a glimpse of myself in the mirror. My hair sticks out in every direction as I have spent most of the night trying unsuccessfully to negotiate a comfortable position. Together with the thick black circles under my eyes, I remind myself of one of those before and after mugshots released by the American police departments to warn against the long-term effects of Methamphetamine abuse; needless to say, I currently resemble the after picture. I grimace and turn off the light, as if that will improve the appearance of my visage. It does. My reflection is cast in shadow, but behind me a movement catches my eye. I pause, straining in the mirror, watching the space behind my shoulder. The empty dining room is still. I'm breathing hard, skin prickling in the cold air but my face is burning. Slowly I turn and walk out of the bathroom, seeking anything out of place in the silent shadows. Each panicked breath is illuminated as a white cloud in the darkness and I realise that I feel as cold as a grave.

Feeling distinctly less brave than I am trying to act, I tread carefully into the small hallway linking the dining room and lounge, casting a look up the narrow stairs as I do and pausing momentarily to check for movement. The soft orange glow from my bedside lamp allows me to see that the small space between my bedroom at the front of the house and the tiny nursery at the back of the house is empty. I move on into the lounge, which at first appears jet black. I shift my eyes about the room as they adjust to the dark and I can make out the small couch to my left, the fireplace on the far wall, a small tv next to the sash windows at the front of the house.

Finally, the front door to my right, which I approach giving it a gentle push to ensure that it is shut. It is. I am shaking hard. Listening for a few seconds more, I tell myself it was just a trick of the light, a glimpse of something imaginary in the corner of my eye.

After a moment longer shivering in the dark, I retreat back up the stairs, breathing hard with the effort of hefting my weighty frame and dodging obstacles all the way. I climb into my bed, wincing as it creaks ominously under me and restart the process of attempting to find a comfortable position, which requires much sighing, pillow rearranging, shifting and swearing. With a pillow wedged between my knees, lying on my side to face the window, I finally find my halcyon state and sigh blissfully, as sleep rushes up to greet me.

Several seconds later I feel a wetness growing between my thighs.

"Oh for f... argh" I cry into the darkness struggling to sit up in bed. Pulling back the covers and turning on the light, I try to see the damp patch drenching through my jim-jam trousers, but I can't because the bump is in the way. I sob quietly and consider just ignoring it and attempting to get a bit more sleep. It can take hours with a first pregnancy to even get to the point where you need to head to the hospital, I reason. Even as I do so a searing pain tears through me. I tense, leaning back on my arms and trying to focus on deep breaths and not panicking and in doing so I lose track of how long the contraction has lasted.

It feels like an hour passes, I have no concept of time. As it starts to subside I reach for my mobile and dial the taxi company number I've programmed in. The phone rings, sounding unfeasibly loud in the quiet of the night. The cold is sinking through my skin again and I pull up the duvet to try and stop my shivering. Finally, a groggy voice answers the call. Taxi hastily booked, I look up my Dad's mobile number. Quickly finding it in my favourites, my hand hovers over the call button, hesitating. A second contraction is brewing, I can feel it building. I put the mobile to sleep and throw back the covers.

The taxi arrives long before I have struggled into my maternity jeans and waddled down the stairs. He waits patiently. I can hear him stomping his feet outside my front door, fighting off the cold. As I open the door another contraction quivers through me and I barely manage to hand him my bag as I double over. Luckily it turns out that Zaf has two children of his own and so he is completely unfazed, holding out his arm to support me as I shuffle out to the cab. Climbing in the back, mid-contraction, is unexpectedly painful and I lean back in the seat clutching my bump, feeling that at least one challenge had been completed but worse is to come.

As the pain subsides and the Astra (which I now realise smells a bit kebab-y) rumbles to life, I look up at my little house. I'm not sure why, but my eyes are drawn to the window of the front bedroom. In the blur as the car lurches forwards, I gasp as I glimpse what appears to be a face, eyes jet black, lips turned, grimacing down at me through a crack in the curtains. As we speed through the dark streets, I suck in panicky breaths, my mind racing and attempting to make sense of what I have just seen. But then I am lost in the next contraction and I spend the journey focusing only on the pain that tears through me.

"Your first one is it love?" asks Zaf, looking back at me in the rear-view mirror. I nod frantically, pain rendering me incapable of speech. "It's always a bit of shock the first time. I remember when the missus had our first. What a palaver!" he chuckles.

"Nargh..." is all I can manage by way of a response.

"Don't worry love, we'll be there soon. Lucky for you it's the middle of night. No traffic innit." He grins at me over his shoulder.

"Breathing through the pain...isn't working...isn't helping" I manage with a shaky voice. Zaf lets out a proper belly laugh.

"Nah love, you want drugs innit! Get the proper stuff as soon as you get in there. If they think you've gone too far, they might not give it you. Happened to my sister that. She nearly decked the midwife," he chuckles some more, "Was alright in the end mind."

"Jesus Christ!" I shout, as a fresh contraction hits. My hand is gripped tight on the door handle as I squirm in my seat, trying to find a way to get comfortable. Apparently Zaf finds this hilarious and I want very much to punch him in the face. By the time we reach the maternity ward of the grandly titled, but mildly decrepit, Royal Hampshire County Hospital, Zaf has proffered yet more of his sage fatherly advice and I have to focus very hard on not telling him to fuck the fuck off. It's not that it's not great advice or that I'm not grateful, but I am in no state to appreciate him waffling on at me.

    He offers to walk me into the maternity unit, but I decline for his own safety and shuffle my way to the drab hospital wing. The grim little brick building resembles an Eighties office block and a gaggle of nurses huddle against the cold outside sucking on cigarettes. I expect one of them to spot me and dash off to fetch a wheelchair while the others comfort and care for me, but I am dutifully ignored as I walk past them, stopping occasionally to clutch at my belly in agony whilst glancing at them desperately hoping they will notice me. They huddle closer and talk louder so my groans of pain can't be heard. How incredibly rude!

    To make matters worse, some utter bastard has placed the maternity ward on the first floor so when I've made my way through the automatic doors I have to stand waiting for the lift or face the agony of climbing the stairs. The corridors are brightly lit by strip lights but empty. I look around me, hoping to commandeer a passing nurse with a wheelchair, but nobody comes. Hobbling into the lift, I wince as it jerks upwards. Every tiny movement sends a fresh wave of pain through me.

    Following the signs through the maze of corridors, I descend on the buzzer to the maternity ward, jabbing it with relief. The voice that rumbles through the entry system seems nonchalant as I explain my situation. I slump into a seat in a little waiting area as I wait for someone to come and save me. Taking a brief respite from the pain of my contractions, I close my eyes, a short pause before the storm hits.

    The door to the ward swings open suddenly and two midwives bustle out, quickly bringing me to my feet and sweeping me into the ward. I barely have the chance, to ask after my wheelchair. What is it with this place? The next ten hours are a blur; kind faced midwives with reassuring words, ask if there is anyone they can call for me. My response is the same every time; no, I'm on my own I gasp, quickly adding an urgent request for an epidural. Each successive midwife smiles at me in a nauseating manner and assures me I'm too far gone for that now. Why are you lying to me? I think to myself.

By the time she is born, I am broken, exhausted and frantic. The wave of relief as she leaves my body is delicious but does little to lift my spirits, which seem to have sunk without a trace. I lay on the hospital bed, legs suspended in the air in stirrups, panting for breath as a plucky midwife holds my baby out for me to see. Wrapped in a standard issue hospital blanket, my wearied brain struggles to reconcile this tiny pink alien with the bump that had grown within me all these months. Huge, wet blue eyes blink at me as I lay limply in the bed.

"It's always best for baby and Mummy to have skin contact as soon as possible." says Nurse Plucky as she strips back the flimsy blanket that had been covering my top half and wedges the baby against my naked breast, before I can protest. I place a limp arm against her back and close my eyes.

Somehow, I drift into a shallow sleep, waking when the midwives take the baby to examine and then return her to my side. By the time the doctors had finished with my vagina, which I sense is in tatters despite their best efforts, I am too hungry to sleep.

"Tea and Toast?" Nurse Plucky offers. I wonder briefly if this damnable women will ever go off shift, but I nod gratefully, feeling a full English would be much more appropriate under the circumstances. If pushing a tiny human out of your foo wasn't enough to justify the calories, I don't know what is. Said tiny human is by this point sleeping peacefully in the Perspex crib beside my hospital bed, which seems a little unfair as I have done all of the hard work and barely slept in the past forty-eight hours. Ingrate. If this is what Motherhood is about, I'm beginning to have serious doubts about this particular life choice too. More orderlies arrive in the little delivery room and inform me that we were being moved onto the ward.

"But what about my tea and toast?" I say miserably.

"We'll make sure it gets to you," the orderly is a young man, with black tattoos snaking up his neck from under his uniform. Heavily jelled, black hair falls into crystal blue eyes as he pushes the bed along the corridor. His mouth tilts into a friendly smile under his heavy beard. I blush, suddenly aware of my state of undress and then feel immediately ashamed of myself. Hussy, I think, you've literally just given birth for Christ's sake. I try to put this uncharacteristic flooziness down to the effect of too much gas and air, but in reality, I just don't feel like myself.

CHAPTER SIX

The midwives wake me at four am and then again a few hours later; sleep deprivation to help prepare me for the sleep deprivation to come. They assure me that I need to wake baby to give her a feed, but my body is telling me the only thing either of us need is sleep, a need constantly denied to me by a howling baby in the next ward. Shortly after the sun has risen someone sweeps across the curtain to my cubicle, and I see that there are three other women with their babies on the ward. Opposite me and to my right are empty spaces where I suppose other mothers would be deposited when they have finished giving birth. Grateful for the relative solitude I turn my back on the other inhabitants to face the window, trying not to notice their side tables full of cards and magazines, and the occasional bobbing balloon announcing "Congratulations!". Outside the winter sun is bright and the sky a crisp flawless blue. I wonder, without really caring, if it is going to snow.

By the time the breakfast trays arrive, I am just settling off into a pleasant doze, and although desperate for the rest, my body is famished and after silently cursing the absence of anything even remotely resembling a Full English breakfast, I devour the meagre offerings quickly, hoping to snatch a few more minutes rest before the baby wants another feed or change. She starts kicking off just as I am shoveling the last mouthful of vaguely unspecific foodstuffs in. Shit. Can she hate me so much already? I lift her out of her Perspex crib and place her on the cushion on my lap and we began the painful and frustrating process of getting her latched on. I have been told by everyone who had an opinion on the subject that breastfeeding is not painful if you are doing it right. What bollocks, I think as the toe-curling pain rips through my right breast, but at least she is getting fed.

Just as I am settling her down into the crib again, a bed is pushed into the ward by a gaggle of nurses and carers. The woman on the bed looks pale and tired but chats cheerfully with them as they slide the bed into the space opposite mine. The woman looks much older than me, or so I think having neither had nor wanted the chance to see how I look in the mirror today. Her short blond bob is matted and stuck to her head with sweat and her cheeks are red, perhaps from the interminable heat of the place. It feels like a sauna and I'm grateful to have a bed next to the window, where the tiniest slither of ice-cold air slips through a small gap I have been able to negotiate with one of the late-night carers. The crowd disperses, having settled in their patient and I realise that there is no Perspex crib and no baby with this woman.

I'm trying not to stare, my own tiredness succeeding over my curiosity, as the woman sits with her eyes closed, propped up in the bed. Wondering idly if there is some kind of post-birth babysitting service no one had told me about I slip into a gentle snooze. It's a curious thing attempting to sleep on a busy ward while people are constantly milling about you talking in hushed (and sometimes not so hushed) voices. You quickly get a sense for when someone is approaching you, as opposed to the squeaky shoed approach of a nurse as they flit around. I reluctantly prize open my eyes when I sense someone near my bed and I'm surprised to see the woman from the bed opposite standing by my baby's crib, looking down at her with a smile on her face.

"Oh, sorry did I wake you?" she whispers as I struggle to sit up straighter in the bed. Her voice is gentle but has a slightly high pitched, squeaky quality.

"Its fine," I croak and reach out for a glass of water.

"She's so beautiful," she gushes, I studiously avoid looking at the lump in the Perspex crib, "What's her name?" I shrug. With everything that has been going on I haven't even given it a single thought. "Oh well" she continues reaching into the crib to stroke the baby's hand "plenty of time for all that!" I manage a weak smile, but I just didn't have the energy or enthusiasm for small talk.

"My baby is in NICU" she adds, "she's a bit poorly but the doctors say she's going to be ok. My husband, he's popping by soon, wants to call her Eve after his grandmother. It's a beautiful name, don't you think?" she doesn't pause to give me the opportunity to respond, but I nod, it is a beautiful name. "She's really tiny. Only 4lbs, even though I carried her to full term. The doctors aren't quite sure why yet, but they're running some tests. Anyway, I'm hoping someone will come and take me up to see her soon. It feels really odd having had a baby but not having her with me. Wish I could've had a cuddle before they took her away. Do you mind if I have a cuddle with your little one?"

"No, go for it." I say, relieved, thinking maybe if she needs a change, this woman will do it for me. She was enthusiastic enough for the both of us. Settling my head back on the bed, I feel my eyes begin to droop, but she isn't finished talking.

"She is so sweet. Look at these little fingers! It's visiting time soon I think. Who's visiting you today?" I reluctantly prize open my eyelids with tremendous effort to see she is smiling sweetly down at my baby. I wonder if she would notice if I responded at all.

"No-one." I answer grateful I have been able to stop my voice from wobbling.

"Oh. That's a shame. Well, I will keep you company until my hubby gets here at least. Oh, look she's yawning. That's so cute! I cannot wait to have cuddles with my little one. I hope they don't want to keep her in too long. I really need to get back for my other two. I've got my big boy, Alfie, he's nine and my little girl, Molly is six. They are so excited to meet their baby sister. Do you have any others?"

"No." I say. I'm not being short I just don't have the energy. I hope she doesn't think I am being rude, I'm just struggling to keep my eyelids up. She doesn't seem the type to need the input of a second party to keep a conversation going. I wonder if her husband is enjoying the brief peace and quiet and immediately feel awful for being so mean.

"In that case, you need to make sure that you sleep

when baby sleeps." She continues, "No such luck for me! I'm going to be running around after the other two while Eve is sleeping. Not that I mind, it's such a wonderful time when they are tiny like this. You should make the most of all the cuddles you can get. When they get older you have to catch them first!" she laughs so loud my baby starts to wriggle in her arms. "Oh! She is waking up. Would you like to hold her?" she holds the baby towards me.

"No, thanks. Can you just pop her in the cot? Sorry I've just got to pop to the loo." Slowly like I've aged three hundred years overnight I pull myself off the bed and shuffle off the ward to the toilets, leaving the woman to deposit my baby back in her crib. They don't warn you that after you have given birth your body is left with considerably more blood than you need and the body disposes of this superfluous fluid, largely by making you piss like Niagara Falls and sweat buckets in the days preceding the majestic process of giving birth. By the time I have shuffled back onto the ward, visiting hour has started and the ward is filled with more than the allowed quota of enthusiastic visiting relatives bustling around each bed. Except mine. I pull the curtain around my bed and lay back down, falling asleep in seconds.

When I wake the ward is eerily silent and assuming I have miraculously slept through the visiting hour I creep out of bed and pull back the curtain. The bed opposite me has the curtain pulled shut, but I can tell there are several people crowded into the small space by the hushed voices. The rest of the woman on the ward sit silently on their beds, all eyes are turned on the cubicle opposite mine, some holding their babies close. I sit in the chair next to my bed and strain to hear what is going on. A female voice is talking calmly and slowly in a sympathetic tone. I heard the words "we did everything we could" and "I'm so sorry", followed by a loud guttural sob. After several more moments, a sombre faced, female doctor with red ringed eyes appears, closing the curtain tight after her and walks off the ward. The woman in the bed opposite me cries for hours. Nurses come and go, but the sobs don't stop all night. Not loud dramatic sobs, but a quiet, helpless moan that seems endless.

Later a doctor comes onto the Ward and pulls the

Ward sister to one side, but within earshot of me. He informs her that the woman has to be moved. The nurse nods in agreement but implores that she is still in shock and refuses to be moved and so the sobs from behind the curtain continue for many hours more. Eventually a man, face blotched and eyes sore, appears from behind the curtain and with eyes cast firmly downwards walks off the ward. All I can think is that he doesn't look the kind to be married to the woman in the bed opposite, though I can't articulate why. Whilst stooped now, I can see he is tall and thin and in all the time he has been on the ward with his wife he has not uttered a single audible word.

The crying from behind the curtain has now stopped and I assume that she must be sleeping or sedated. I watch all of the other mums as they cuddle their newborns a little tighter, faces cast down, their guilt at having a child that survived is obvious. My baby stays in her cot though and will stay there until I am forced to feed or change her. Sleep, feed, burp, change, eat, repeat. I manage to catch a passing nurse, as she leaves the enclosed bed opposite me to ask when I might be able to leave. She says she will send a doctor over to check me over and I take that as a sign I might be released today. I start to pack up my things and lay out the winter baby grow ready for our departure, before easing my bruised body into my maternity jeans.

By the time the Doctor has arrived I have fallen asleep yet again on my bed, and I wake to find the curtain has been pulled back on the bed opposite and the woman is lying on her bed, staring at my baby's crib. The doctor checks our notes and informs me we are good to go. I pluck my baby out of the crib and begin the process of wrestling her into her fluffy babygrow, not noticing the woman opposite has risen from her bed.

"Would you like a hand?" she asks in a quiet voice with forced cheerfulness. She is raspy from crying and she looks like she has shrunk several inches into herself, as if the joy had been sucked right out of her.

"Erm, yeah. Sorry, I haven't got a clue what I'm doing." I stand aside. With seemingly military efficiency she puts the requisite limbs into their allotted holes and poppers up the baby grow.

"One last cuddle?" she asks lifting the baby off the bed before I have a chance to answer. I wasn't going to deny her it. I wanted to know what had happened to her baby but thought it a rather obvious question and didn't want to put her through the heartache of having to explain it to a stranger out loud. Watching her as she gently squeezed my baby with more love and affection than I felt, for I felt none at all, I wondered briefly if it would be out of the question to ask her if she would like to keep my baby. Here she was desperate to feel the warmth of her newborn in her arms and here I was desperate to avoid having any contact with mine. I wanted to tell her, keep it, I don't want it. Instead, I waited until she handed her back to me, feeling like an ungrateful wretch all the while.

Carrying her in the nook of my right arm, with my bag slung over my left shoulder I walk off the ward and downstairs to where my father is waiting. He places a kiss on my forehead and enthusiastically lifts the baby out of my arms for his first cuddle with his granddaughter. He gently informs me that I look like shit as we walk to his car. I sleep the whole journey back home and it is only when I look back up at my little house, I remember what I had seen the night before as I had driven away in the taxi.

CHAPTER SEVEN

Over the course of the next few days I soon come to realise that I am to become a full-time slave to the tiny pink tyrant that I have unwittingly created with my own genitals. Sleep, feed baby, change baby, eat (food that is, not baby) and repeat. I suspect that she is actually a very easy-going child and manage to get considerably more sleep than the baby manuals and midwife that visits us seems to think is normal. Exhaustion still torments my body and mind though, and whenever I'm not performing some kind of baby related duty, I curl up on the sofa and doze, always waking disorientated and still unfeasibly exhausted.

When the midwife, Jen arrives for a second home visit on the fourth day, she seems dismayed that the house and I are still in a disgraceful state, although she doesn't say as much. There are boxes stacked up in the dining room from where I had moved in two months ago and simply haven't found a space in my little house for them. Jen offers to make us both a cup of tea and I hear a suppressed gasp as she enters the kitchen, perhaps from the days of stacked dirty dishes and baby paraphernalia scattered across the counters. Feeling a pang of guilt, I hear her run the tap to wash up some cups, as I change the baby's nappy for the tenth time that day. The contents are a lurid orange, runny and smell distinctly vinegary but I have given up wondering if that is normal or not.

Domestic duties addressed, Jen returns with two steaming hot cups and places them down on a side table.

"So, how is Mum doing today?" she asks as she

unpacks the baby scales onto the carpet. Being referred to in the third person as Mum is irksome, but I'm getting used to the way these healthcare professionals so often feel the need to talk to me like I am the child. I'm sure she feels that she is here to help me, but in my eyes she is the enemy who has infiltrated my barracks.

"Fine," I say running my hands through my slick, greasy hair, "just tired." She looks at me then, very closely. I attempt a sanguine smile, which I hope also passes for charming. Her lack of smile in response suggests I have failed.

"Okay...and how is the breastfeeding going?" I grimace. She's caught me out already.

"We had to give up." I try to hide the sheer relief I am feeling that that particular ordeal is over. While the constant churn of cleaning bottles and making up feeds is a monumental pain in the arse, I'm happy to put the pain and stress of breastfeeding behind me. I suspect that the baby had been hating it as much as I had. "She was just so hungry all the time, so I started giving her formula and now she won't breastfeed at all."

"Right well, breast is best." I steel myself for the lecture that is inevitably coming. The NHS, it seems, takes an almost military stance where breastfeeding is concerned. I understand the benefits, of course, but on top of everything else, it's just too much for me. I justify this to myself by deciding that doing what is best for me, would inevitably also be best for the baby, surely? I'm not being selfish. I'm just a realist.

"I will try to keep up a feed or two a day" I promise before she can launch into a lecture on the relative benefits, but I have no intention of doing anymore breastfeeding whatsoever. The midwife regards me suspiciously and nods. Having weighed the baby, she sits back in the armchair and silently fills out her paperwork with copious notes in wild looping handwriting. I watch her as I sip my tea, triumphant in my little victory and try to read her erratic handwriting upside down. Meanwhile, the baby lies on the floor, kicking her legs out and staring into space.

It's an unnerving process to have a stranger come into your house and assess your ability to perform a task which has been undertaken by billions of women throughout the history of mankind. The majority of them having done so without a midwife, whilst squatting in a mud hut without running water or sanitation and not even a Silvercross pushchair to lighten the load. Although, I reluctantly admit to myself, even the poorest mothers in the worst conditions generally do have some kind of partner and most likely a motherly figure to support them throughout the process. My tired mind wonders briefly how different things would be if my mother was here. Would she have been with me at the hospital? I certainly think she would have visited with cards and flowers and balloons, like the other elated grannies I saw on the ward. I like to think she would have come to visit on a daily basis, delighting at her little granddaughter while I jumped in a hot bath or stole a couple of hours of undisturbed sleep. I stop that train of thought before the melancholy takes hold. I can't have the midwife thinking I'm feeling down. She will think I'm not coping.

"Have you decided on a name yet?" Jen finally asks with a warm smile. I've been expecting her to ask from the moment she arrived. I meet her eyes and wonder how long she has been watching me so closely.

"No. I'm just too tired to think straight." I blow the steam from my cup and slurp noisily, watching her watching me over the top of my cup. This is a battle of nerve and wit, which I'm pretty certain I am currently losing.

"Sorry, do you mind me asking? What is the situation with the father?" she asks brusquely. I'm taken aback. I hadn't expected that one. How incredibly rude!

"We're not together anymore."

"And is he involved with the baby in anyway?"

"Nope." She seems surprised at this and makes a few more notes. My anxiety is building. Last I checked there wasn't a law against bringing up a baby by yourself, so why is she making me feel like I'm doing something wrong here?

"Ok, do you have any support? Close friends, family...?"

"Nope. We're doing fine, honestly. Just tired, but that's normal right?" She looks dubious.

"It's perfectly normal, of course. But most new

mothers have a network of support to help them through. Does your Mother live nearby?" I sense she is trying to help but she is just getting on my nerves.

"No, my mother died when I was very young." I say with an impatient sigh. Jen blanches at that.

"Oh, I'm sorry." She says and I shrug. "Ok, I think you would really benefit from coming along to a weekly group we run up at the Harvest Church for new mums. If anything, it would be an opportunity to get out of the house and meet other new mums from the area. There is a weighing station. Baby is a tiny bit underweight at the moment, so it would be good to try and weigh her more regularly. Just to keep an eye on things." I nod trying to seem enthusiastic. The idea sounds hellish to me, but I suspect this is the only way I will be able to convince her that I am coping. And I am coping. Just in my own unique, dysfunctional way.

"Okay." I say, "Sounds like fun." I realise I've gone too far and she thinks I am being sarcastic, which I am a little. Jen is not amused.

"I know you're tired and believe me, I know it's tough, especially when you are on your own." I wonder if she has any clue just how impossibly difficult it really is. I doubt very much that she does. Prim little Jen probably has a delightfully middle-class husband and a semi and a 4x4 and a perfect brood of well-adjusted children. Bully for her, I think bitterly. "But it's really important that you get out and about when you can." There is sense in what she is saying, but I am so weary I cannot comprehend how this could possibly help me. I just want her to be out of my house. Since she arrived, all she has done is scrutinise me and my house and the baby. Her pinched features scream disapproval. I know that my house is a mess and more importantly that I am currently a mess, but I could do without this sanctimonious judgmental windbag coming into my home and telling me what is best for me.

I don't know if she can sense my bristling or if her visit has just run its course, but she starts to pack up her things. We both look up as the unmistakable sound of footsteps, slowly crosses the ceiling above us. I feel cold to the bone suddenly and I shiver.

"Have you got someone visiting?" Jen asks cheerfully as she slings her bag onto her shoulder.

"No" I say, fear twisting in my stomach, "it must be coming from next door".

"Oh, I was sure I saw someone in the window upstairs when I arrived...must've been a neighbour's house" she adds with a smile. "I'll pop by in a couple of days, just to see how you are getting on." she says brightly as she steps out of the front door.

"Ok, thanks. Bye." I start to close the door.

"Oh and do give the Mum and Baby group a try. It's tomorrow at ten!" she calls as I hastily shut the door. Leaning with my back against it, I look up to the ceiling and listen. The house is silent. Despite the anxiety growling at my chest I walk up to the front bedroom, knowing that I will find the room empty. The house remains silent and the room is exactly as I had left it; disheveled chaos.

Downstairs, I climb back on the sofa curling up, abandoning the baby on the floor on her play mat. Before I close my eyes, I notice something in her hand. Leaning closer, I reach out and pluck the thin strip of red wool out of the baby's clenched fist.

CHAPTER EIGHT

The next morning, I wake feeling a bit lighter and driven by the fact that my own smell is starting to bother me, I decide to treat my fetid skin to a shower for the first time in a week. The warm water feels divine against my grubby face and I'm instantly more alive and awake than I have been since the baby gate-crashed my life. Stepping out of the shower I can hear her starting to grumble from the lounge and I fling on clean clothes for the first time in days. Feeling fresh and renewed I decide I will go to the Mum and Baby group, if anything else to prove to the nosy midwife that I am coping and, also more importantly, so she will stop harassing me.

I walk into the kitchen to heat up the baby's bottle and even I am shocked by the scene of devastation. Dirty dishes fill the sink, even dirtier laundry is piled up against the washing machine and several full nappy bags are stacked on top of the overflowing bin. Best not to overdo it, I think to myself, plopping the bottle into the warmer. I decide I need a hearty breakfast to steel myself for what is to come, but the cupboards are bare and so I pull a tub of ice cream out of the freezer; there's no shame in Ben and Jerry's for breakfast. Tucking in to scoop the melted bits from the edge of the tub, I resolve to get out of the house as soon as possible, before the urge to clean becomes overwhelming. I reassure myself that it is against the rules to do any housework before baby is over one week old, especially when you are doing it by yourself. In fact, make that before the child is at school full-time if you are doing it all by yourself. The key to setting achievable goals is to keep it realistic after all.

Back in the lounge the baby is really starting to kick off. Keen for the neighbours not to report me to nosy midwife for child neglect I hurry in with the bottle. Propping her in the nook of a corner cushion, I hold the bottle to her mouth and sit beside her on the sofa. Her greedy little hands grab for the bottle and she closes her eyes, sighing contentedly as the warm milk flows. I reach for the remote control and zone into This Morning, feeling myself start to nod off as some third-rate celebrity drones on about a magical children's book they have written. I wake to the sound of the baby sucking up the dredges from the bottle and commence the burping ritual, again nodding off halfway through. My mind and body are yearning for fresh air. The walls of this house are starting to feel stale and imposing.

I wrap her up in her winter baby-grow and hastily pack a bag with the collection of baby crap that now needs to accompany me wherever we go; nappies, bottles, spare clothes. It weighs a tonne. Looping it over the handle of the buggy, which I have struggled to erect for the first time outside the front door, I turn to grab the baby just as the buggy dives to the ground, dragged down by the weight of the bag.

"Oh for f..." I shout. A hand shoots out of no-where and grabs the handle. The arm attached to it is tattooed with thick black gothic letters.

"Need a hand?" A deep voice asks. I step out of the front door to meet my saviour who is stood in the front garden of the house next door. Oh wow, I think before I can strap a harness onto my brain, he is beautiful. His dark hair is clippered short, the kind that looks like it is fun to stroke all over. Light green eyes, that are nothing short of stunning, regard me with a hint of a humour. He seems familiar, even though I'm certain we have never met. Or at least I'm hoping he hasn't met the greasy haired, saggy maternity clothes wearing version of me with the distinct fug of a woman who has let her personal hygiene standards slide into the gutter. Freshly showered me is distinctly more pleased to see him. He is still leaning awkwardly over the little wall that separates our tiny front gardens, preventing the pram from crashing to the ground, with a cheeky, lopsided grin.

"Thank you." I say feebly and dash back into the

house to grab the baby, leaving him standing there; I need a second to compose myself. Reappearing seconds later, I place the baby in the pram, her tiny weight just the right counterbalance.

"Got it?" he checks as he stops steadying the pram. He's looking at me with an intensity that is thrilling but I am becoming painfully aware of the burning feeling spreading across my cheeks.

"Yep, thank you." I say and still avoiding his gaze hurry down the path away from him. When I reach the end of the road, where the huddled-up terraces intersect with the larger grander houses, I look back, under the pretense of checking there were no cars coming before I cross the road. My heart sinks slightly when I see that he has gone. I'd rather hoped he'd been so mesmerised by my beauty and guile that he had stood and watched after me. Clearly not.

Walking fast through town, it takes a while for my cheeks to cool under the gentle sting of the icy fresh air. And by the time they have, they are starting to warm up from the exertion of pushing the pram up the hill. I have spent too long cooped up in the house and I can feel myself sweating underneath my winter coat. My muscles start to complain. At the top of the hill, I turn towards the Harvest Church, where I am confronted with a long row of buggies, parked neatly along the wall. Suddenly nervous, it occurs to me that I hadn't expected there to be so many other mums there. I count at least twenty prams and the urge to turn around and go home is overwhelming. I feel a thick ball of tension forming in my chest as I consider the what ifs: what if I drop the baby in front of everyone, what if no-one talks to me, what if I say something stupid (let's face it, that one is inevitable, I have form), what if the midwife decides I'm not fit to be a mother and takes my baby away. I consider momentarily that the last what-if wouldn't actually be so bad and allow myself to consider life returning to normal; first and fore-most getting a decent night's sleep. I instantly feel awful for thinking this and hate myself a little more.

Despite the nagging ache in my chest, I force myself to carry on up the hill. Each pram I pass causes my heart to thump a little harder and by the time I reach the entrance I'm feeling sick. Wedging my tatty second-hand buggy into a small gap, I shift the bag across my shoulder and lift the baby out of the pram. A wall of heat hits me the second I walk through the automatic door and I am instantly desperate to peel off my coat, certain that my face is flushed a deep red again and a sheen of sweat has gathered on my forehead. Looking around, I see the reception desk is empty and there is no indication of where the mother and baby group is, so I reluctantly follow the general commotion down the corridor. I soon find the room. The door is closed and only has a small window high up so I cannot see the pandemonium beyond. Nervously I open it and look in.

The noise amplifies immediately, and I am overwhelmed by the sound of about two dozen chatting mums, plus roughly the same number of squalling babies. Brown chairs (the stackable kind you normally find in village halls that can rarely accommodate a normal sized bottom) are placed in large circle in the middle of the room. In the centre, the floor is covered with brightly coloured baby mats, some with arched play centres dangling over the top of them. Babies are sprawled out all over the mats, some on their fronts attempting feebly to prop themselves up, others lying wriggling on their backs and a handful crawl in amongst the crowd. Mums, and one decidedly anxious looking Dad, sit on the chairs nursing their teas and coffees, chatting idly with one another. To my right, on a row of tables there is a changing mat and some weighing scales. Jen looks up as she is helping one of the mum's wrestle her screeching offspring out of its baby-grow. She spots me and I register the surprise on her face before she can cover it with a smile, holding up her index finger, she calls out "I'll just be a minute!"

I nod and look around the room for an empty chair. Spotting one in between a blonde mum who appears to be having a doze in her chair and the anxious dad, I make a beeline, gratefully plonking the baby onto a brightly coloured mat. I shrug off my coat and whisper a shy hello to anxious dad who offers me a thin smile in response. He is too busy watching his offspring like a hawk to engage in conversation and that suits me just fine. To my left, snoozing mum lets out a gentle, snorting snore.

Hope

"Lovely to see you Tess." Jess announces loudly, directly into my left ear as she squats beside me having crept up with the stealth of a jaguar. "I'm really glad you came." Her hand curls around my shoulder like a claw. I attempt to give her what I hope passes for a genuine smile, but say nothing, not wishing to encourage her to stay and chat. "Well, help yourself to a tea or coffee, there's some biscuits too I think." she points over at the refreshments table as I try to stifle a yawn, "And we have a weighing table over here so you can see how baby is getting on. Other than that, meet some of the mums and if you have any questions come and grab me." She pats my shoulder and heads back to the scales where a panic-stricken mum is frantically mopping up her baby's effluent.

I ease myself back into the hard-backed chair, made more uncomfortable by my bottom over-spilling the edges. I'm desperate for a cup of coffee, but don't yet feel comfortable enough in my new surroundings to walk across the room to get one, so I just sit and watch the scene around me, silently craving caffeine and solitude. Most of the people in the room are deep in conversation and from the snippets I pick up, the general theme seems to be sleep and poo. I hear more than one mum utter the immortal words "God, I'm tired". For the most part, the mums are fairly normal, dressed in jeans and tee-shirts with hints of vomit or less palatable baby fluids.

I spot amongst the regular mums, an odd woman who appears to have confused the Mums and Babies Group for the Ascot Races, wearing approximately 2 inches of makeup, including mascara so thick her eyes are in danger of welding shut each time she blinks. Her skin-tight dress frames her size six figure perfectly and the only thing missing from her ensemble is a ridiculous hat. As her little one flips and starts a commando style crawl, she hops up, gingerly tiptoeing amongst the pink fleshy baby pile in her stiletto tipped Jimmy Choos, to the horror of the other mums who watch on aghast. Retrieving her renegade son, who had been eagerly attempting to climb over a slightly smaller baby, she clambers back to the edge of the baby pile miraculously without skewering any of the infants on her ridiculous heels. The room lets out a collective sigh of relief.

"Do you fancy a coffee?" someone says through a yawn and I realise the woman to my left has woken from her nap. She looks at me lazily and yawns again, revealing several black fillings. I decide immediately she is my favourite person here, mainly because she is offering to bring me caffeine.

"Yes please." I'm gagging for a coffee and could cry with happiness, but I don't. She slinks off, hitching up her sagging maternity jeans on the way and returns with two plastic cups and a couple of bourbons. She offers me one and we sit munching in companionable silence.

"I'm Sally by the way." She spits out a few crumbs as she speaks.

"Tess" I say spitting out a few crumbs myself.

"First time?" she asks. "I haven't seen you here before."

"Yep," I gulp down the last of my biscuit, "The midwife was getting antsy about me spending so much time alone at home."

"Alone? What about your other half?"

"He's too busy shagging some slag called Suzy" I reply, too tired to think of a more socially acceptable response. Sally throws back her head and laughs. It's been a while since I've heard a laugh like that and it feels good.

"Sounds like a bit of dickhead to me." She says and I nod.

"He is. I haven't spoken to him since the day he walked out. He blocked my number." I was telling her more than I would normally feel comfortable with, but it felt cathartic to be getting it off my chest with this stranger. I start to feel a little at ease for the first time in months.

"You're better off without him. My first husband was the same, he just couldn't stop himself. He reckoned it was some kind of psychological disorder. Like he was addicted to bonking slappers. He must have thought I was a complete halfwit. Knobhead."

"I am glad to be rid of him..." I say inwardly wincing at my lie, "but it would be nice to have a bit of support."

"You'd spend more time cooking his tea and washing his pants than he would help out with night feeds and nappies.

Trust me. I'm on my third."

"Husband or baby?" I ask.

"Both!" she says and we laugh. "Although I managed to get rid of hubby number One before we had any kids. Thank God! I had two babies with number Two. We just grew apart. It all ended very amicably. Now I'm with number Three and it seems to be going well, touch wood." Sally taps her head. I wonder where she finds the energy for three kids, much less three husbands. I'm pretty certain I couldn't muster the energy to start from scratch with a new relationship, but then I remember the rather lovely neighbour who came to my rescue and suddenly I'm not so sure. Calm yourself Tess, I think, you've only just met him.

The general noise in the room grows as the Mums start to collect their offspring and head towards the door, chattering the whole time. Apparently the group is over already. I must have been very late because I've only been here for ten minutes at most.

"Fancy grabbing a coffee? They do a mean Panini in the cafe here." I consider for the briefest moment my dwindling bank account, which needs to be eked out until I have sorted a new job, married a millionaire or won the lottery. I do have a rather handsome, five figure sum in my savings account from the sale of the house and what's left of Mum's trust fund, but I can see that easily being frittered away in no time. As soon as I get back to work I'm going to need every penny as a deposit for a house or I will never be able to get back on the property market. I did consider taking the maternity allowance but it seemed wrong to take benefits with all that cash sat in my accounts. Dad tried to convince me that I had paid taxes and National Insurance my entire working life so I was completely entitled to claim, but it just felt wrong to me. Had I not bashed my ex-husband over the head with his own stapler, I would have received maternity pay in addition to a big redundancy pay-out and I wouldn't be breaking into a cold sweat every time I used my debit card. In the end I just think, fuck it why not, and then feel a guilty rush at the self-indulgence.

"Okay, sounds good." We collect our babies. She tells me hers is called Poppy, her third daughter. I tell her I haven't gotten around to naming mine yet, but she doesn't seem particularly concerned, unlike stroppy midwife who had acted like it was the end of the world. Wheeling our prams in from the cold, we deposit the babies in the corner of the cafe which is empty except for us, and sink into a large leather sofa, sipping our coffees and sighing happily. At least being out of the house meant I wasn't living in a constant state of guilt over the things I should be doing but wasn't.

"So, have you always lived in Alton?" asks Sally.

"No, I'm originally from Winchester. I used to live near Guildford with the Whiney Shitlord, my ex-husband" I clarify, Sally grins. "I moved here to be far enough away from him, but close enough to my Dad, who still lives in Winchester."

"Ahh, makes sense. Alton's alright, not much for shopping, but it's a nice place to live. Lots of good schools too. Whereabouts are you?" she asks.

"I'm renting a little cottage on Grove Road." She nods, so I assume she knows where that is.

"I love those little Victorian terraces. So cosy. You know they tore down loads of those little cottages in the seventies during the slum clearances. Such a shame, but I guess it wasn't cost effective to modernise them. Much cheaper to just tear them down and fling up a housing estate"

"They are cosy but ridiculously impractical. My only bathroom is downstairs." She looks aghast and I'm embarrassed by my humble living conditions, so I try hastily to shift the topic of conversation to her. "Do you live in Alton?" She nods her head, as she gulps down her mouthful of coffee.

"I'm up on Normandy Street, up the top of town by the train station. James works in London so it's handy for him. It's one of the three storey Victorian houses just off the main road. Beautiful inside but I'd kill for a driveway!   God!   I never thought I would be dreaming of a bit of off-road parking!"

"I feel your pain," I say, "I'm too scared to move my car. I don't think I would ever get my space back ever again." Her pained expression shows her solidarity.

"I just love older houses: the character, the fireplaces,

the sash windows. Not so keen on the ghosts though!" she laughs and I can't tell if she is being serious. My mind is pulled involuntarily back to the night the baby was born and I feel the skin prickle on the back of my neck. Sally spots my mood has soured and laughs again. "You don't believe in ghosts do you?" Ah, she was joking.

"No, not really. Well, certainly not during the day." I say, "I'm a little more open minded at night." I peel off the edge of my chocolate pastry and pop it into my mouth and as I reach out to pick up my coffee cup, I notice a small blob of chocolate on the edge of my finger. As I raise my finger to my mouth, Sally squeals at me.

"Don't!" she scrunches up her face in disgust as my hand hovers close to my mouth.

"What?" I freeze, my finger close enough for me to reach out my tongue and lap up the chocolate, which I briefly consider doing.

"Right Tess, I am going to give you some advice which might one day save you from doing something utterly horrific. I'm going tell you about a game, known in my house simply as Nutella or Poo." Suddenly I know where this is going and I jerk my hand away from my mouth.

"Exactly," she says, "When my eldest was a newborn, I decided to partake of a mid-morning crumpet smothered in Nutella. Breakfast of champions. I was naive back then and full of joy for the world, so when I saw what I thought to be Nutella on my hand I decided to lick it off, forgetting that I had very recently done a nappy change."

"Oh God."

"Needless to say, it was not Nutella." She says earnestly and I manage a look of deep sympathy.

"Okay, so how do you play this game?" I ask, raising my coffee cup to my lips to try and hide my smile.

"You just sniff it first, that's all."

"That's...revolting." I sniff my finger tentatively and realise it is in fact chocolate. "It's safe" I say licking my finger.

"Heed my words!" Sally says and we both laugh, our voices echoing around the empty cafe.

It's funny how sometimes you meet someone and it

instantly feels as though you have been friends for years. It feels like that for me and Sally and we end our lunch exchanging mobile numbers and vowing to meet up regularly and unlike most opportunities for social interaction, I actually savour the prospect. By the time I leave to walk home the sun has come out in full force, so I take off my coat and push the pram down to Alton pond so I can enjoy the warmth of the day. It's not far from The Harvest Church, nestled between the train station on one side and large blocks of newly built flats on the other. In truth it's not much to look at; wide and plain with a scattering of sultry ash and elm trees leaning inward.

I walk alongside the bank of the railway line, the ponds meandering edge to my right. There is a small bungalow further up the track, nestled at the base of the high bank that carries the train tracks. Its garden runs alongside the path and is divided by a low white fence with flaking paint. It feels for a while as though I have intruded into the little house's private garden and I try not to notice the greying underwear flapping in the wind from the washing line balanced precariously between two poles.

Further along, the path veers to the right and the left hand-side is dominated by a tall, modern building, small balconies spotted across the wall, all of which are empty. I'm at the halfway point around the water's edge so I park the pram and sit for a while on a bench, letting my lazy muscles take a short break and watching the ducks and swans bobbing on the water. A dark shape on the opposite side of the lake catches my eye. It looks like a woman, she is dressed in a large full skirt that billows out around her and tight-fitting top, both solid black. She seems to be looking directly at me. I cup my hand over my eyes against the sun to get a better view. She is stood on the opposite bank of the pond, so close to the edge I am sure that her toes must be sinking into the silt and the water lapping at the leather of her boots.

The baby grumbles in her pram and I look away momentarily. When I look back, the woman in black is gone.

CHAPTER NINE

The next day I wake feeling groggy and bad tempered after a bad night with the baby. I'd hoped today's appointment with the midwife would be my last but that depends on her assessment of how I am coping. Given how I feel, I'm relieved that I had attacked the housework with renewed vigour after my lunch with Sally. The sink is empty and clean, the floor cleared of dirty washing and the bin has been emptied for the first time in a week. I'm wearing a clean bra for the first time this month – always a major achievement!

The baby, however, has a different plan and just as I settle onto the sofa with a fresh cup of coffee, ten minutes before the midwife is due to arrive, she decides to empty the contents of her colon all over her nappy, which in turn leaks all over her clothes. The mess is so horrendous it takes most of an entire pack of baby wipes to clean her tiny body. I have just taken her poo stained clothes out to the washing machine, held at arm's length on account of the horrific smell when the doorbell goes. The baby still lies on the change mat, completely naked and nappy-less as I open the door, flustered and unbeknown to me, with a long smear of baby shit across my temple and in my hair.

I usher Jen in as she surveys the scene of devastation around her and I try to explain about the explosive turd-maggedon. She smiles, while wrinkling her nose at the vinegary aroma and reassures me that she sees things like this all the time. But something about the way her eyes are squinting as she looks around the room, suggests that she is distinctly unimpressed with me. I offer to make her a cup of tea, in a feeble show of having my shit togetherness, which she accepts, before setting about the process of weighing the baby. When I return to the lounge, she is just poppering up a fresh baby-grow. She sits up into the armchair behind her and plops the baby on her knee.

"Everything ok?" I ask, placing her cup on tea on the table beside her. It's one of the little antique mahogany jobs I pilfered from the house before Matthew could get his grubby mits on it. The large dent I put in its edge with Matthew's driver still makes me smile.

"Her weight is starting to catch up, which is good." Jen says this while examining the back of the baby's head, stroking it gently, "are you still trying to breastfeed?"

"Err...no. She refused to take anything but the bottle for days now. I did try." I say, avoiding looking at her.

"Ok, that's fine. I'll make a note. Have you had the chance to give her much tummy time?" she asks.

"Sorry, I'm not sure what you mean?"

"See...here, "she turns the baby so I can see the back of her head, which is completely flat, "sometimes when the baby has spent too much time lying on their back, they get a bit of a flat head. It's perfectly normal but laying her on her front for short periods of time will help her build up the strength in her neck too."

"Oh." I say, silently seething. I'd spent hours getting the house in shape and she hasn't said a word about that. She was straight in with the criticism. I am beginning to think I can't get anything right. "I'll try to remember." She looks at me and smiles. It is, I suppose, meant to be a gesture of reassurance, but jarred with her telling me off I don't smile back.

"And how is mum feeling today?" she says placing the baby on her playmat on the floor and taking a sip of her tea.

"Fine. We had a rough night last night, but I'm finally catching up with the housework." I gesture around me and Jen regards the room without enthusiasm or remark.

"It must be hard without a partner to support you. How would you say you are coping?" I do not like this line of questioning, particularly as I have made a herculean effort to get the house in order. Is her remark suggesting that, in her opinion, I am struggling to cope? I think for a second, deciding what to say, whilst simultaneously worrying that my lack of response will be telling. I try to muster a convincing smile.

"I think I'm doing ok...she's still alive" I make a ta-dah motion with my hands. The midwife is not amused, and the grin slides off my face. "Why? Don't you think I'm coping?" I say sounding a tad petulant, which is not what I intended. This is not going well.

"I didn't say that." You didn't deny it either I think as she takes another sip of her tea. "We just like to check that all of our new mums are getting along ok before we discharge them to the Health Care visitors."

"Sorry? The what now?"

"We'll schedule another four visits from Polly, our Community Health Care Visitor. She'll check in on you to make sure everything is ok."

"Do you do that to all the mums?" I ask.

"Yes, it's standard procedure" she replies but I think that she is lying.

"Ok well..." I say getting ready to stand and show her out.

"Have you much planned for the rest of the day?" she asks pleasantly, her cold eyes regarding me.

"Uh, well apart from the usual, you know nappies and bottles and all the rest, I was thinking about popping out this afternoon for a walk."

"That sounds nice." She replies, "Are you meeting with any of the other mums from the group?"

"I have Sally's number and we are going to meet up again soon, but not today." Jen nods slowly.

"Tess, can I make an observation?" she asks. I tense up like I've been given an electric shock. No, I think, you bloody can't. But this charade is all about giving a convincing act of a Mum who is coping. Mums who are coping, don't tell judgmental midwives to fuck off, so I just shrug, and she continues. "I haven't actually seen you holding your baby. Is everything ok?" What the hell is she implying? I spend all day, everyday day waiting on the greedy little tyrant, which involves holding her plenty. I've had enough of this nosey cow bag and her idiotic questions.

"Everything is fine. I spend plenty of time holding her." I snap.

"How much time do you spend cuddling her?" she asks, her voice is gentle, but it seems like a fake kindness to me. She is trying to slip me up and I'm not having it.

"Hours...every night before bed and after feeds. It feels like I never put her down." Jen seems dubious, but to my relief seems to take my word for it. After scribbling down her notes, she packs up her things and heads to the door. Before she steps out into the cool crisp morning, she hands me a card.

"Well, this is my last visit. If you have any problems or want to talk anything through with me, please don't hesitate to get in touch. My mobile number is on there so you can call anytime." She pats my arm in a way that seems disingenuous and I force a tight smile.

"Thank you" I say swinging the door shut with just a little too much enthusiasm. I am furious. As I run through the discussion we have just had, I quickly draw the conclusion that this woman thinks I am not cut out for motherhood. She'd only invited me to the Mothers and Babies group so she could keep a closer eye on me. I wouldn't be surprised if she was sat out in her car watching me now. I peek a look out the bay window in the lounge and strain to look up and down the thin road, cramped with cars. I am surprised to find that she isn't there. At least, not in sight anyway.

All the while my indignation rages, there is a little voice in my head that says, what if she's right? What if you are not doing a good enough job? What if the baby would be better off with someone else? What then? In my unsettled state of mind, I cannot find an answer to these questions and it is sheer frustration that urges the warning prickle of tears. The room seems to darken around me as a I turn and regard my child, lying on the floor. How can something so tiny and benign make me feel so inept?

Though the day had started bright and clear, the sky is now overcast throwing a grey light over the little room and faced with the prospect of another gloomy afternoon stuck in the house, I hastily text Sally to propose a quick coffee in town. She responds straight away to say she is stuck with the mother-in-law who was imparting her worldly wisdom on the joys of motherhood but adds that she should be able to escape in an hour or two. Deciding that the baby could do with a bit of fresh air, I endeavour to get us out of the house with the nice wholesome trip to the local library. My plan is to do a bit of research on the cottage and its history and I have decided that the library is a good (not to mention free) place to start. Perhaps I could feel a little more at home here if I knew more about its past or maybe get some answers about the strange things I had seen, but more than anything, it is just an excuse to get out of the house without spending any money.

Outside the air is cold and crisp, winter is settling in with ruthless efficiency, but my cheeks are still burning with the effort of pushing the pram through town and within five minutes I have peeled off my coat. When I step through the doors of the library building on the outskirts of town I am suffocated by the heating, forcing me to peel off my winter jumper, leaving only a slightly saggy maternity top, with built in flap for ease of access which would only be useful if I were still breastfeeding. It had started life a crisp white colour, but now is yellowing, particularly around the armpits. I make a mental note not to raise my arms, on account of the fact I havn't shaved under there for at least nine months and the shrub-bage underneath has become fascinatingly revolting.

I approach the lady behind the counter and she regards me serenely from behind her computer. I wonder why it was that librarians, above all others, always seemed to have their act together. This lady had chestnut brown hair in an immaculate bob, neat standard issue librarian glasses and a face that is both wise and suspiciously line free.

"Can I help you?" she asks in a quiet, steady voice.

"Umm... I'm not sure," I say pushing the buggy to the side of the desk so that I can get closer to the desk and avoid being overheard, "I'm trying to do a bit of research about the history of my house. Do you have records of who owned local properties historically? I was hoping to go back to the late eighteen hundreds or early nineteen hundreds?"

"No, I'm afraid we don't have anything like that. Have you tried looking on one of the genealogy websites?"

she asks. "You can access them for free from one of our computers." She guides me across to a set of tables set back to back, with a row of three computers on each side. Positioning the pram, with my (thankfully) sleeping baby next to me, I sit in the chair, while the librarian logs me in and pulls up a website.

"If you access the census information, you can search on address. There are censuses going back to 1841 and as recent as 1901 available on this site. While you are doing that I will go and have a look in the local history section. I have a feeling we might have something up there that will help you." She smiles and walks away, disappearing up a set of stairs at the other end of the room.

I feel a buzz of excitement as I enter the address of my cottage into the website and click search. At first it seems to take an age, but then a page of results fills the screen. I scroll through the 1901 census results, deciding at the bottom of the page I might need to go back a little further, I select 1890s from the list. Clicking through the results I am directed to a facsimile of an ancient looking document, filled with elegantly sloping handwriting. I realise that this is not for Grove Road. It takes an element of luck and perseverance to find the results that I am looking for.

When I do find number 14 of Grove road, there is the name Mary Donoghue. According to the census she was a spinster, aged 52 and living alone. Her occupation was given as Laundress and her birthplace Cork, Ireland. Feeling disproportionately pleased with myself and enthralled with my discovery I smile to myself, even as I acknowledge this information doesn't really tell me much at all. The librarian returns with a book in her hands, laying it down on the desk beside me.

"Here it is. This is a compilation of photographs of the town comparing the old with the new. If you're lucky you might find a photo of your house in there." I beam up at her.

"Oh, wow. Thank you so much!" she offers a neat smile, before leaving me to browse hastily through the book. Each Page is filled with grainy black and white photos, contrasted against the modern comparisons, and a brief description detailing the changes through the years. I vaguely recognise some of the buildings from my long walks around town during the final weeks of pregnancy. Others are completely alien, even among the "modern" photos which, judging by the extraordinary number of bubble perms and shell suits, must have been taken back in the eighties. Right at the back of the book, is a picture of my house standing exactly as it does to this day. I skim the description, which indicates that the original photo had been taken around 1860.

"Get in!" I say a little too loud apparently. I see the person at the computer opposite peer around the screen at me.

"What's that then?" he says and I look up to see my handsome neighbour that saved my pram from crashing to the ground smiling at me. I flush bright red.

"I found a picture of my house in the book." I'm looking down at the book, to avoid looking at him and getting even more flustered. If I make eye contact with him, I might lose it completely. He must think I'm the dullest person on earth for getting excited about an old picture of a house. What a loser!

To my dismay he gets ups and walks around to look at the picture over my shoulder.

"Cool" he murmurs. He smells fantastic. I try not to make it obvious I'm sniffing him like a weirdo, whilst thoroughly enjoying his musty aroma. "I love these old photos."

"Are you into history...and stuff?" I ask not daring to tear my eyes from the page even as he moves back to his seat opposite me.

"Yeah, I think it's interesting. I love old buildings."

"Me too. Sorry am I a bit tragic and dull?" he shakes his head vigorously. "I just wanted to know a little bit more about my house." I look up and notice his beautiful green eyes looking back at me. And there's that cheeky grin again. He really is rather lovely to look at. I'm trying not to stare and seem obvious, but I fear that my flushed cheeks are betraying me somewhat.

"I've got a book like this at home, if you ever want to borrow it, just pop round." He says. I allow myself to make full eye contact with him and my stomach somersaults with the thrill of it. He can't be flirting with me, surely? No, he's just being kind and friendly I decide. Beautiful men like him don't flirt with single mothers that they barely know. In fact, that's it. He doesn't realise I am single and that must be why he feels so comfortable talking to me. I relax a little knowing the pressure is off. I don't have to impress him, but I'm loath to admit I am more than a little disappointed. Not wanting him to see my confidence falter, I smile up at him, aiming for friendly but not too friendly.

"That's really kind, thank you." I turn back to my computer and attempt to look busy. He dithers awkwardly for a second, apparently thrown slightly by my brusque response, and then walks back to his computer. Cursing myself for being utterly shit, I log off the computer, drop the book back with the prim librarian and make a hasty exit, realising as I shiver in the nipping December air that not only has my dishy neighbour been confronted by the sight of me in my manky, yellowing maternity top, two small dark circles have appeared around each of my breasts where I have leaked milk. Shamefaced, I set off towards the coffee shop.

CHAPTER TEN

Sally throws back her head and laughs as I pull my jumper back down to cover up the damp patches on my top.

"Don't." I say grinning, "It's not funny!"

"Yes it is!" she says, still sniggering. We are sat in the front corner of the coffee shop, the long glass shop front stretched out in front of us, allowing us bask in the dying winter sunshine.

"I don't know why I even care." I admit sipping from a coffee cup that is so large Sally's face is completely obstructed from view as I lift it up to take a glug.

"Oh, I think you do," she says with a wink, "It's not a sin. You are allowed to have romantic liaisons post baby, you know?"

"I'm sure I am," I reply, "but one-week post baby, seems a bit...umm...ambitious?"

"I'll admit, you're probably being a tiny bit premature, but there's no harm in a bit of flirting."

"I think I've probably scuppered any chances of romantic liaisons. There's no point even aiming for friendship. He doesn't seem the type to want to listen to me whining about how goddamn tired I am. Or the colour of my offspring's latest poo." Sally grimaces.

"Always with the poo," she sighs, "Okay, fair point. I still think you should take him up on his offer to borrow that book. But, try and wear something a little more alluring. Just in case the flame of romance hasn't been entirely extinguished by Leaky-Boob-Gate." She takes a mammoth bite of her chocolate brownie, crumbs tumbling down onto the head of baby Poppy, who is nestled happily against her chest.

"I don't have any alluring clothes that fit me anymore. Not without the aid of a girdle and I'll be honest, I don't think my bladder could take the pressure anymore. So, make that a girdle and incontinence pad combo. How very enticing!" We cackle again, this time waking my baby, who has been sleeping in her buggy. Her tiny face puckers into a silent howl, as if she is practising for the real thing. I sigh and pull a bottle out of my bag. Tucking a greying muslin under her chin, I slip the teat into her mouth and she suckles greedily. Leaning over the pram at an angle is already making my back hurt, but I tell myself I simply don't have the energy to take her out and hold her. Even though I know she will need winding afterwards. I look up and catch Sally watching me with a curious look on her face, which she quickly flips to a smile.

"Want another?" she asks placing her sleeping baby into the pram and picking up her empty cup. With my free hand I drain the dredges of my gigantic cup and nod enthusiastically. I sense the air between us has grown suddenly awkward, although I'm not entirely sure why. Whilst I feel closer to Sally than I have to any other human being since my husband walked out on me, I'm worried what she thinks of me. I worry, generally, what everyone thinks of me. I always have, but becoming a single mother had never been my intention. Whilst I personally hold no preconceptions about the type of person that finds herself alone raising a child, I know there are still plenty of people who do. That is why I still wear my wedding ring, not that anyone seems to care either way. I know that Sally can't possibly think badly of me for being a single mother, she'd been there herself and she was a kind, empathic person. So why the strange looks, I wonder. I must be doing something wrong, but I'm not sure what.

By the time Sally has returned with the two fresh cups, I have lost my appetite for company. We chat pleasantly as I drain the steaming hot coffee as quickly as I can without burning my mouth. I am suddenly feeling exhausted, I explain and rise to leave. Sally gets up from her seat and wraps her arms around me in a friendly hug. Enveloped by her warmth and the comforting scent of her vanilla-y perfume I close my eyes for a second. All thoughts of her hostility evaporate instantly, and I leave my friend feeling comforted and calm. My suspicions had been just that. I decide I need to check my paranoia in future. As I walk back to the house, I look up to let the warmth of the afternoon sun drench my face, a contented smile playing at the corners of my lips. Arriving home, I change the baby's nappy and settle her in the moses basket in the lounge, curling up on the sofa with a thin woolen blanket over me.

  I'm woken by the sound of my mobile vibrating on the table beside me. It feels like I have been asleep for just a few short moments, however the room is now dark and cold, and the baby is fidgeting grumpily in the crib. Picking up the mobile, I almost drop it again when I see the caller id. Matthew is calling me. Staring at the screen, I fail to decide what to do before the call goes to voicemail. Heart beating fast in my chest, I place the mobile back down, watching eagerly for the notification that a voicemail has been left. The phone jumps to life as the message registers. Not quite ready for the first interaction with my estranged husband in nearly nine months, I leave the phone while I fetch a fresh bottle from the kitchen. Lifting the baby out of the crib I place her in the corner cushion, sitting beside her while I hold the bottle for her to drink from. I tuck a blanket close around her as she feeds, resolving to get the first fire of the season going as soon as she is finished.

  In the silence of the room, all I can hear is my own thoughts urging me to pick up the voicemail and find out why he has contacted me. I reach out for the tv remote and switch on the news, but my mind struggles to focus. At first, I imagine him sat in his car, having left her, reaching out to find me so that we can be together again. A flutter of hope fizzles and dies in my chest; I refuse to let myself get sucked in that easily. Next, I think of them together, lying side by side in bed, him running his hands through her thick long hair, stroking her face as he had once done to me. They talk and laugh, smiling into each other's faces and then they kiss the slow lingering kiss of lovers. He is moving on top of her, slipping between her shapely legs. When they have finished making love, she asks him if I had been a good lover and he laughs and says "God no! Honestly, you have no idea". In my head they have fast forwarded several months and she had a big curving belly that he strokes lovingly and kisses tenderly as she smiles fondly down at him.

I wonder if this fantasy could have been my reality. Could I have tried to be less of a social pariah, so that he could have been proud of me? True I couldn't have stopped the miscarriages, but I have proven now that all I needed was a little more time. If only I could have tried a little harder, he might have stuck around long enough for us to have had the family we so desperately wanted. It seems no matter how I cut it, the end of my marriage was entirely down to me. Having talked myself round to the crux of my situation, I felt prepared to listen to his message, half anticipating that he has accidentally butt dialed me and the recording would just be several minutes of muffled noises and nothing more.

As I'm about to press the button, a gentle knock at the door surprises me and I almost drop the baby's bottle. She cries out indignantly as I prise her off the cushion and into the nook of my arm. Picking up the bottle, I open the front door.

My neighbour is stood in the doorway, looking sheepish, a book clasped in his hands.

"Hi," he smiles at me. It's a glorious smile and my body reacts warmly to him. I'm sure my cheeks are reddening.

"Hi!" I say, popping the bottle into the baby's mouth to prevent any grumbles.

"I just wanted to pop round that book for you," he holds it out and looks down at the baby, "sorry is it a bad time?"

"No," I say wedging the bottle under my chin, giving me a Jabba the Hut chin and enable me to take the book from him. I study the cover to avoid meeting those beautiful green eyes again, "thank you that's really kind."

"I'm Tom by the way" he smiles leaning against the doorway.

"I'm Tess" I say looking up shyly. The aim is coquettish but I'm pretty certain I still look like Jabba the Hut. To my own surprise I add, "Would you like to come in for a cup of tea?" He looks behind me over my shoulder.

"Oh no, I don't want to interrupt, if you and your

husband are having your tea or whatever..."

"It's fine, come in." I say moving to one side as he steps in, "My husband and I are separated, so it's just me...and the baby."

"Oh, sorry, I wasn't meaning to pry" he's clutching his hands awkwardly in front of him as if using them as a shield. Is he suddenly feeling vulnerable now he knows I'm single I wonder? I could have badly misjudged the situation and my cheeks burn with embarrassment.

"Don't worry, its old news" I'm flustered and hoping I don't sound like a bit desperate. The silence between us grows a little awkward so I say "Here, you finish this and I'll grab us a cuppa." The look of sheer panic on his face makes me smile, as I hand the baby and bottle over to him, but he cradles her with an ease that suggests it isn't the first time he has fed a baby.

In the kitchen I start to panic, realising I am still wearing my scabby maternity top, although now it is thankfully covered up by my tatty holey jumper. I look down at myself; oversized jumper that I stole from Matthew which has seen better days, saggy maternity jeans and the whole ensemble finished off by mismatched socks one with a fetching pattern of green ducks and the other with a cartoon panda face on it. I'm not about to score a modelling contract, unless the advertising campaign is "End Poverty". As the kettle takes an age to boil, I begin to fret over the state of my lounge and pray that there are no festering nappy sacks loitering about the place.

When I return, Tom is stood studying the contents of my bookshelf, with a muslin on his shoulder as he gently pats the baby on her back. She belches and spits up milk onto him. My ovaries ache and I immediately want to breed with this surprisingly fatherly man.

"Shameful." He says as I place the tea cups down on the side table.

"What's that?"

"Your music collection." I stand beside him following his gaze to a small section of the bookshelf, mostly dominated by withered paperback novels, but with a small selection of CDs wedged against the edge of the shelf. I'm a bit embarrassed to be honest, but in my defense, Groove is in the Heart is a cracking record. I hope he is a fan of Nineties Electric Dance-pop, although his reaction so far suggests otherwise. "Not even a Joshua Tree." He mutters.

"The U2 album?".

"Yes, everyone should have a copy. It is an epic album. A modern classic. Hang your head in shame!" His grin is playful.

"I'm dreadfully sorry, my ex must have taken it. The scoundrel!" I spot the Spice Girls Greatest Hits album amongst the slim collection and point to it, "Yeah that's definitely my ex's. He'll be missing that one." I pluck it out and fling it onto the sofa behind me, "I should probably send that back to him. In fact, I specifically recall him mentioning that he wanted custody of this in the divorce." Suddenly it seems important to mention both that I am divorced and indicate that my ex is a bit of a bell-end. Tom chuckles causing the baby to bob up and down in his arms. His presence feels intense and I need to step away. His closeness is making me feel slightly manic.

Spotting the book where I'd placed it on the arm of the sofa, I pick it up again and look at the cover. Tom holds the baby out for me. "Oh, can you just pop her down on the floor on her play thingamy please." I say, barely looking up from the book. Suddenly I'm an awkward fourteen-year-old girl again, unable to meet the eye of the object of my desires. He places her carefully down, taking care to support her neck and then sits on the floor, cross legged beside her. He holds out a finger for her to grasp and smiles down at her.

"Do you have children of your own?" I ask, my gaze flickering up from the book constantly but then shifting away before he can catch me looking at him.

"Yeah," he says, "two boys". I wonder if he is too engaged in smiling at the baby or if he is just avoiding looking at me.

"They must be very quiet!" I say with a nervous laugh, "I've never heard them."

"They live with their mother." He adds quietly. There is yet another awkward silence between us for a while and I turned my flushed face to the book, not quite sure what to say to him.

"Thanks for this, by the way." I say and he finally looks away from the baby and straight at me. His gaze is intense and I feel naked under his scrutiny. Not in a "dog eying up a sausage in the butcher's window" kind of way. Or worse an "I wonder what your insides look like" serial killer kind of way. He could be in a gallery appraising a painting, trying to understand why it has caught his eye and why he cannot look away. Nobody has ever looked at me like that before and my anxiety melts a little.

"Oh, it's not a problem. I just came across it this afternoon actually and thought I would pop it over while I still remembered." He disengages his finger from the baby's vice-like grip to take the handle of the tea cup as I hold it out for him. "Why are you so interested in the history of this house, if you don't mind me asking?"

"I'm just curious really." I say. It feels like a lame answer and seized by an urgent need to not seem vacuous so I continue, "I've always been interested in social history and old buildings. I guess there must be a reason why I felt so drawn to this house and I wondered if there was anything interesting in its history. It's strange to think it has been a home to so many different people and different families and their lives would have been so different to ours. I just find it interesting really." I'm nervous that I've said too much and come across as a bit dull.

"And have you found anything interesting yet?" he seems genuinely curious, which surprises me.

"Not really. All I know if that at one point there was a Laundress called Mary Donoghue living here. Not terribly exciting!"

"What, the Mary Donoghue?" he's leaning forward now, eyes keen with enthusiasm and I feel a niggling sense of unease.

"I guess so. That was the name on the census anyway. Was she famous then?" My skin is prickling and I'm not sure why. Is it just me or is the room a little colder all of a sudden?

"Not famous. Infamous. She was a notorious Baby Farmer. She was thought to have murdered at least ten children in the town, perhaps a lot more in London and all over England. It's the bloodiest chapter in Alton's history. Tess, are you ok?" He starts to get up and places his cup down before kneeling in front of me.

"I'm...I'm fine. Sorry...I..." the room is swimming around me and I take a deep breath to try and bring everything into focus. Tom's face, earnest and concerned, hovers close to mine, his hands gently gripping my elbows as I sway.

CHAPTER ELEVEN

That night I sleep with the baby's moses basket on the bed next to me, although in truth I don't sleep much at all. I wake often, even when she is sound asleep, groggily lifting myself up to peek over the side of the basket and check she is okay, slipping a finger behind her neck to check she isn't too cold or too warm. By the time she does wake for a feed, I am drained and irritable.

Tom had finally left after my hearty protests of not having eaten much that day. He'd insisted on making me an omelette first and then watched me like a hawk as I ate it without appetite, then he'd left. I couldn't remember the last time I had eaten a proper warm meal since the baby had been born, but I didn't tell him that. Reassured that I had regained a healthy colour, Tom had scribbled his mobile number onto a scrap of paper and insisted that if I had anymore funny turns, that I call him immediately. Had I not been in a state of suppressed shock, I would have been elated at his gentlemanly gesture.

Instead, I feel on edge. The house seems hostile and cold. We retreated to the bedroom after he had gone, where I'd spent the rest of the evening on Google horrifying myself with the history of baby farmers. In a time before adoption or formal orphanages, baby-farming had become an extremely lucrative trade. The women involved, often seemingly respectable middle-class widows and spinsters preyed on down and out single mothers, who faced a stark choice; the workhouse or starve on the streets. So, when they saw an advert in the local paper for a childless couple looking to adopt a baby, for a small maintenance payment, they jumped at the chance for their child to have a more comfortable and stable upbringing.

The babies would often be drugged with laudanum to keep them from crying out in hunger. Baby-farmers like Mary Donoghue, however, had decided the venture was much more profitable if she was to murder her charges. It was believed that she operated in Alton for a short time, perhaps only a matter of months, during which period ten tiny bodies were discovered in the town, usually in the river or by the pond with a scrap of red wool tied tight around their necks where she had strangled them. It was believed that she had travelled into London, where she had advertised for children to adopt, returning with them at night to her little cottage on Grove Road. It was only when she had started to flaunt her accumulating wealth that people in the town had started to grow suspicious. Donoghue had fled before she could be captured by police and presumably moved to a new town to restart her venture afresh.

This was all information that I could have lived without knowing and only deepened my anxiety. It was ridiculous to believe that the ghost of a Victorian baby-farmer was lingering in my home, but I couldn't shake the unease and decided that I would make an effort to get out of the house tomorrow. Waking after what feels like a few minutes sleep, we go through the routine of dressing, washing and packing the baby's bag with all the standard paraphernalia. I am mightily impressed with myself to have us in the car before nine am, particularly as it has taken a ten-minute battle to wrestle the buggy into the boot of my little hatchback; it feels like a major victory to me. That is until I find myself sitting behind the steering wheel without a single clue as to where we are going. I consider briefly just driving, but the silent protests of my dwindling bank account remind me that I cannot afford to spend a fortune on petrol. Instead I decide I need to be somewhere familiar, somewhere that feels safe; we head for Winchester.

It isn't until I drive past King Alfred's statue, the imposing bronze statue with his back turned onto all entrants of the city and see the high street stretched out, lit up by a hundred strings of lights that I realise it is nearly Christmas. I park the car in a gloomy, underground car park in the centre of town. As soon as I have parked the car, I pull out my phone and flash up the calendar app. I barely know what day of the week it is most of the time, yet it still comes as a shock to realise that there is just one week until Christmas Day. This time of the year has always been sacrosanct for me and I always used to make a huge effort to have the house in order, filled to the brim which tinsel and everything sparkly. I'd spend hours foraging for holly and ferns and pine cones for my wreath which would adorn the front door from 1st December until late January (I never could bear to take the thing down). Christmas day itself had always been split between my Dad's (I couldn't bear to think of him being alone at Christmas) and Matthew's parents, but ultimately ended with us curled up by the fire at home, watching the usual old tripe on tv.

I wonder what kind of Christmas he will be having this year without me. It occurs to me that I now have to somehow recreate the Christmas cheer and buy presents on a severely limited budget and for the first time in my adult life my festive enthusiasm ebbs. Pushing the buggy through the shopping centre, hung with dramatic sparkling Christmas lights, I am forced to accept that the day trip has transformed into an impromptu Christmas shopping trip. Stopping in at the nearest high street coffee shop for a festive flavoured skinny coffee with an extra shot, I summon just enough enthusiasm for a bit of shopping. The sugar and caffeine combo would normally act like rocket fuel, but I'm so wrecked it's more like a timid kick up the bum that only just managed to get me moving again.

Without much of a plan, besides to buy Christmas stuff, I meander in an out of shops, looking blankly around me but ultimately buying nothing. I have no idea what I need this year. Most of my budget used to be eaten up buying crap for Matthew, that he never appreciated. Sometimes he would help me out by telling me which book or aftershave he wanted, but for the most part I was stumbling around in the dark and I always was crap at buying gifts. Who do I even need to buy for this year, I wonder? Just Dad and Aunt Sophie, I guess. Do

I really need to buy gifts for the baby?

On a little side street just off the High street I find one of those trendy mum shops, where you can buy the latest in maternity fashion, significantly overpriced baby-grows in every conceivable colour and a collection of plastic toys, also delightfully overpriced. Whilst buying a Christmas present for what would be my two-week old baby by Christmas day, seems utterly ridiculous, not buying at least one present feels a bit mean. I mentally calculate my bank balance (post Mocha) and how long it would potentially last if I bought a few toys. It would be lovely to actually spend some money on myself for a change, most of my cash these days seems to go on nappies and formula. By the time I have reached the back of the shop I have abandoned any hope of finding a sale section and I go about lifting up the all small toys I can find, examining the price tags and then putting them back with an exaggerated sigh. She is only going to dribble on them, so I resent forking out twenty quid! Per toy!

As I riffle through dejectedly, I become aware of a noisily enthusiastic couple that has entered the store and are browsing the maternity wear section. The smell of Matthew's characteristically overly strong aftershave assaults my nostrils before they are close enough for me to recognise their voices. I turn my back to them, sneaking a look over my shoulder. Matthew is wearing a dark grey suit with his tie loosened off. He is stood behind Suzy with his arms wrapped around her tummy, which had blossomed into a tight little bump. She is dressed in a bright red dress that clings to her figure, a neatly tailored black coat hangs open, too small to fit around her belly. I turn back and examine the toy in my hand, which I have no intention of buying, straining to hear what they were saying, but also frantically planning my escape. So, this is why he has been trying to contact me, I think suddenly remembering the voicemail from the night before which I still haven't listened to. He wants to rub salt in the wound. What a monumental bastard.

I risk a quick glance over my shoulder and notice with horror that they are making their way towards the back of the shop, casually wondering down the left side, with just a small display inbetween us. As soon as they get to the far corner, I swivel the pram around away from them with skill that would have qualified me for Formula One and with my head down rush towards the exit. I don't look back and I don't know if they see me, but to be sure I walk hastily, almost running, back to the car. Despite the baby's protests (it is feeding time apparently) I drive us straight home. By the time we arrive at the house, she is howling, tears streaming down her red chubby cheeks. I am crying too.

Having wrestled the pram and shopping into the house, I am tempted to leave her in the car, but reluctantly open the door to be hit by apoplectic screams. I hold her as we settle on the couch and lower the bottle into her eager mouth. She closes her eyes blissfully, slivers of tears still damp on her face. Sighing through gasping suckles, I feel her tiny body relax into a warm lump in my arms, her fingers grasping for mine as they hold onto the bottle. The house around me is silent and I pull a blanket over us and close my eyes while she feeds. Waking instinctively when the bottle is finished, I shift her onto my shoulder and commence the tedious burping ritual, patting with one hand and balancing her bum with the other. When I think I've safely removed most of the toxic gas, I hold her in front of me, her back rested against my forearms and her fragile little head resting in the palms of my hands.

She looks a little like me, I decide. My Dad didn't have many pictures of me as a newborn it had been an extremely difficult time for him, but I can already see that she has my mouth, my freakishly small ears and possibly my chin too. I struggle to see any of Matthew in her. In fact, I struggle to conjure up his face at all, besides the short glimpse I had seen of him in Winchester, his face was slowly shifting out of focus in my mind. I hope that she will be nothing like him as I stroke my finger across her soft cheek.

Suddenly her face twitches, at first as if she is about to smile and then into a thunderous frown. Her eyes flutter open momentarily and her eyes flit up in their sockets. My heart jumps into my throat, as I assume, she is having some kind of seizure. A loud, deep grumbling noise that emanates from the tiny infant's tummy and as the slow warmth cascading from her bottom spreads across my forearms, a curious light brown colour started to seep through her baby-grow at the edges where her nappy is underneath. I realise what has happened a tenth of a second before the hideous vinegary smell hits me. I laugh, not sure whether to be disgusted or proud, before restarting the seemingly unending process of clearing up the considerable mess that my offspring has created with her bottom.

That night, we take a bath together and having cooked a respectably healthy meal for me, we curl up on the sofa with a blazing fire, contented in each other's company. It occurs to me, as we were getting ready for bed, that I hadn't felt any jealousy when I had seen them together in the pretentious baby shop. I'd only feared that he would see me, because then he would want to be a part of our lives. Of course, if I didn't have my own baby, the whole incident would have been devastating, but there was good reason to be grateful for what I did have. As I tuck the baby into her moses basket, I lean down and place a gentle kiss on her forehead. She regards me with a curious look for a few moments and then eyelids dropping settles into a deep sleep.

I am asleep within seconds of switching out the light, but I dream of a Victorian woman dressed in black, with a sombre dark face and my tiny garden filled with small headstones. The nightmare fades, and I find myself walking through Alton pushing the buggy. Everything seems normal, until a kind faced elderly woman asks if she can see my baby, but as I push back the hood of the pram, I realise that it is empty. I have left my baby at home. I abandon the pram standing on the side of the pavement as I sprint home. I turn down side streets but find myself somewhere familiar yet not. Frustrated I sprint faster through streets that I know the name of but can't recognise, until I realise, I am hopelessly lost. I wake in the dark. The room is cold, but I am plastered in sweat.

CHAPTER TWELVE

The next morning, I am woken by a loud banging at the door. The baby and I have dozed lazily despite the bright winter sunshine obtrusively filling the room. I step out of the bed and peek through the curtains, to see my Father stood by my front door looking up at me, he smiles and waves. Stood behind him is my Aunt Sophie.

"Oh, good God," I mutter, hoping that they can't lip read. I plaster on a fake smile and wave back. Flinging on some clothes, I lift the baby out of her crib and shuffle down the stairs to let them in. When I open the door, my Aunt manages to wrestle herself in front of Dad and flings her arms around us in a dramatic embrace. Sophie was my mother's older sister, and so I'm told, about as different from her as she could be. Where my mother was quiet and reserved, Aunt Sophie was loud and energetic. Where my mother was considered and careful, Aunt Sophie was impulsive and flamboyant. Both sets of characteristics were welcome and whilst I would have loved to have had both women in my life, having just Aunt Sophie was a close second. Even though she was, in my opinion, completely bat-shit crazy.

When I had been about five, I had concocted the strange notion that Aunt Sophie was somehow after my Dad in a romantic sense. She had been spending a lot of time at the house, getting stuck in with the housework and occasionally staying overnight too. When I'd confronted my Dad tearfully about my fears, for I thought she would try and take him away from me, he had laughed so hard he had cried. It wasn't until I was much older and had been introduced to Aunt Sophie's "special friend" Brenda, I had realised why.

"Oh Tess! My dahhh-ling..." she pulls out of the embrace to gaze down at her little great niece, "she's beautiful! Just beautiful! Excuse the intrusion, dear. We simply got fed up of waiting for an invitation!" Aunt Sophie dives in to grab the tiny infant from my arms and bustles into the house. Dad steps out of the cold, closing the door behind him and kisses me gently on the forehead with cold lips.

"How are you doing?" he asks wrapping his arms around me.

"Ok, just tired." I muffle into his winter coat. He pats my back and offers to put the kettle on. I nod and thank him and leave the baby with Sophie so I can hastily brush my hair and teeth in the bathroom. I feel a little more human for a clean and tidy head when I return. Sophie is taking up most of the sofa, her cerise poncho spread all about her, the baby tucked inside with her as she coos and fusses. I decide to sit on the floor under the bay window, opposite her. The ancient radiator pressed against my back, warming me through to my core.

Dad appears with three steaming hot cups, which he distributes before sitting in the little armchair watching with an air of disgruntlement as Aunt Sophie is stealing all the cuddles.

"Where are the bags?" she says suddenly looking up to my Dad, "Give her the bags then." Having only just settled in the chair, Dad grunts with the effort of pulling himself back up. He grabs half a dozen plastic carrier bags that Sophie had ditched at the front door upon arrival and piles them around me.

"What's this?" I ask peeking inside one.

"Some provisions dear. We had a little shopping trip, didn't we Daniel." Dad nods wearily and sneaks me an exaggerated eye roll.

"Oh! You didn't have to..." I start.

"Nonsense! It's not every day your favourite niece has a gorgeous little baby. It was absolutely our pleasure dear." I don't bother to point out I am her only niece as I browse through the bags, pulling out cute (if overly formal) outfits for a newborn, brightly coloured fabric teddies and plastic teething rings. I am certain that between them they had managed to empty most of the shop I had visited the day before. Their "little" shopping trip has saved me a fortune in clothing, and I feel myself welling up with tears of gratitude and relief.

"Oh, don't be silly." Says Dad as he shifts uncomfortably in his chair.

"I'm sorry," I sniff wiping away a globule of snot, "Thank you so much." I get up and hug Dad and then my Aunt, who holds the baby slightly away from me, protectively. Clearly, she is not ready to relinquish her for hugs just yet.

"You know she is just the spit of your mother," says Aunt Sophie grinning down at the little baby who is regarding her with wide blue eyes, "and you for that matter." Dad stands up to examine the baby a little closer before nodding in agreement.

"Not your nose though," he adds, bopping her on her little nubbin, "You have my nose, don't you little one."

"Have you come up with a name yet?" asks Aunt Sophie instantly harpooning the elephant in the room. She regards me severely as though I have neglected my motherly duties (which in fairness, I have).

"Not yet." I reply with a sigh, "I've just been too exhausted to even think about it." Sophie casts a meaningful sideways glance at my father.

"It must be tough, doing everything by yourself." she says placing unnecessary emphasis on the last two words. I nod and Dad clears his throat as if preparing himself to say something. We both looked at him expectantly.

"I umm...I've been contacted by Matthew, by the way." He says and I bristle.

"Oh?" I don't really want to hear about it, but I sense we are going to have this conversation whether I want to or not.

"He said he'd been trying to get hold of you." says Dad.

"He's called me once, but it went to answer phone." I reply, "You haven't told him about the baby, have you? Or where I am?"

"Oh God no," replies Dad indignantly. "I wouldn't do that."

"So, what does he want?" I ask trying to sound like I don't care, which I am increasingly convinced is true.

"I'm not sure. He just said he was trying to get in touch with you and you weren't answering your phone, and would I ask you to give him a call. He did ask for your address, but I didn't give it to him." He adds.

"He probably just wants to let me know that his new girlfriend is pregnant. Just in case I was in any doubt as to whether it was his junk malfunctioning or mine...prick." I say and Aunt Sophie gasps.

"Language in front of the baby! Although you are right, he is a prick." She admits, mouthing the offending word. "Have you thought anymore about telling him about this little one?"

"No. I don't want him anywhere near us." I am firm on that. Aunt Sophie and Dad share a look.

"I don't particularly want him on the scene either, Tess, but how are you going to cope with all of this? Especially when you have to go back to work." says Dad.

"Do you not think I'm coping?" I ask, immediately on the defensive.

"No, that's not what I'm saying," he holds up his hands, "but its damn hard work bringing up a baby on your own. I'm talking from experience. It's not something I want you to have to go through on your own. Especially if you don't have to."

"Do you really think he's going to be interested in my baby, now that him and Slaggy Suzy have their own baby on the way? I think he'd be grateful for me not telling him and what-is-more I'm grateful for him not being told. The last thing I want is that lying toad-faced arsehole coming back into my life, trying to tell me how to raise my baby or constantly undermining me in order to get the upper hand. You know, it's only since he's left that I've realised what a manipulative, passive aggressive, little twat he was to me for all those years. Now I can do whatever I want on my terms without being put down or bullied." I was slightly breathless by the time I had finished my tirade, but I think they got the point.

"Okay, sweetie. Don't get so worked up. It's not good for the baby." Says Aunt Sophie. I notice the baby is starting to wriggle in her arms. As if she was a ticking time-bomb Sophie hands the baby to Dad, who envelopes her in his arms with a proud grin. The flailing limbs settle pretty much straight away, and her little face looks up at him intently.

"If I were him, I'd be gutted to be missing out on this." Dad says almost to himself. Seriously? I think to myself. All the shitty nappies and sleepless nights, days spent wandering around like a zombie after the little tyrant who was still never bloody happy, despite my best efforts. I am sure I am saving him a lot of hassle and stress, and besides, I don't want him swanning in here with his mistress, enjoying all the cuddles and niceness and then buggering off to leave me with all of the crap parts. No, he's made his decision and he will have to live with it.

The room grows silent and I watch Aunt Sophie and Dad exchange a pained look. I sense there is something else coming, the tense atmosphere permeates every inch of the room.

"Your Dad needs to speak to you about something Tess. It's about your Mum." Aunt Sophie nudges Dad unwillingly to raise the subject they have clearly come here to talk about. Dad shifts uncomfortably in his seat. I feel very nervous all of a sudden, as if I know what is coming and I know it is not good.

"Oh. She's still dead, though right?" I crack a smile to attempt to lighten the mood and they both just stare at me. Bad call, I think.

"Listen, this isn't an easy conversation to have and we probably should have had it years ago, but hopefully you will understand why we didn't" he is talking quietly while holding the baby tight in his arms. It strikes me that he looks unbearably sad and I want to hug him.

"Your Dad and I thought it would be best that you knew the truth." Aunt Sophie adds.

"The truth?" I ask.

"Your Mum..." Dad looks like he can't say what he needs to. I've never seen him so wretched as he does right now, "She didn't die in a car crash."

"What?" this is ridiculous, what are they talking about?

Aunt Sophie, seeing my father is struggling pitches in, "She committed suicide Tess." Her words hang in the air.

There are several moments in your life where you will feel as if the rug has been pulled from underneath your feet. The well-established roots that give you a sense of safety and belonging are cruelly uprooted, and nothing can prepare you for the disorientation that follows. If you are lucky it won't happen often, but when it does, you will react on one of several ways; shock, disbelief, anger, refusal to accept it. I briefly experienced all four at the same time creating a storm in my tiny sleep deprived brain. After a short while, I settled for a combination of disbelief and refusal to accept what I was being told.

Dad and Aunt Sophie are studying me carefully for my reaction.

"Oh." I say finally. "Why are you telling me this now?"

"We couldn't explain it to you when you were a child. I mean, it's just an impossible concept for a small child to understand!" says Aunt Sophie.

"And then once the lie had been told, it was incredibly difficult to find the right time to reveal the truth. You can understand why, can't you Tess?" my father looks genuinely pained. As if his lie is a vicious one that he is ashamed to admit.

"Of course," I lie, "but what on earth made you think this was the right time to tell me?" I was struggling to keep it together. Aunt Sophie and Dad exchange another curious look.

"We felt you needed to know. Mental Health problems like this can be hereditary and we were concerned. But more than anything we needed you to know that we were here for you. If, for any reason you were struggling, we would do anything to support you. Anything." Says Aunt Sophie.

"Great so you think I'm not coping." I say.

"No!" they chorus.

"It's more a case of forewarned, is fore-armed." Says Dad. I'm not convinced.

"A lot of women struggle with the baby blues. It's nothing to be ashamed of. We just wanted everything to be out in the open, so if we seem concerned about you, hopefully you can understand why. Your Mum felt the need to struggle on without talking to anyone about how she was feeling. If she had just opened up to us, we might have been able to save her. I'm not saying that you are going to feel the same and deciding whether to have this conversation with you now was excruciatingly hard, please understand. We just needed you to know that if you are ever feeling down, please, please talk to us. We've already lost your Mum..." her voice cracks slightly and my heart softens. I puff out my cheeks and let out a big sigh.

"I'm sorry," I say quietly, "it's a lot to get your head around."

"Just promise us, you will ask for help if you need it." Dad asks. He knows as well as I do how fiercely independent I can be. I guess I got that from my mother too.

"I promise." I say, but I am lying. This is something I need to deal with by myself. As Aunt Sophie stands up to fetch us all another cup of tea, I have a question. It sprints out of my lips before my brain has even had the chance to register it, "How did she do it?" They look stunned and I wonder if it is all that strange a question to ask.

"She drowned herself in the river." Aunt Sophie answers reluctantly.

"Did she leave a note?" They nod. "Can I read it?" They look to each other again. Suddenly it seems important to me that I try to understand this woman better. She is clearly not the person, I had thought she was.

"I didn't keep it." Dad says, he's avoiding looking at me now, deeply concentrated on his tiny granddaughter in his arms. I watch him carefully, trying to establish if he is lying, but my mind is whirling, and I can't. I decide to assume he is lying to me, although I can't fathom why he would. There must be some terrible confession in that letter that he is unwilling to share with me. Maybe she hated me and being a mum and that is why she did it? My thoughts race to a thousand different possibilities, but somehow my first instinct seems the most plausible.

When Aunt Sophie returns with the tea, we all sit in silence, unable to move the conversation on, nor come to terms with what has been said. Eventually, the baby decides to break the atmosphere with yet another explosive poo and Aunt Sophie and Dad choose this moment to make a hasty exit. The baby is irreverently handed back to me at arm's length, their noses wrinkled at the unsavoury smell. As he leaves my Dad hugs me.

"Why don't you come to us for Christmas?" he asks and I'm shaking my head before he has finished his sentence.

"We'll be fine here. Honest. You're welcome to pop by anytime if you want to." He looks over my shoulder at my tiny house.

"The offer is always there if you change your mind." He adds and walks back to the car.

Once the mess in the baby's nappy has been cleaned, I resolve to listen to the answerphone message that Matthew has left for me.

"Hey Tess," that charming voice is so familiar and disarming, "Hope you are well? I've been trying to get hold of you so we can catch up. Could you give me a call when you can? Thanks. Bye."

Jesus Christ, what a disappointment. Although I'm not entirely sure what I had expected. My ex-husband feels like a complete stranger, and for many months he has been exactly that. I suspect that he really did just want to catch up and perhaps to tell me their baby news but can't fathom why unless he just wants to rub salt in the wound. In which case, I decide, I won't give him the satisfaction. He is no longer anything to me and that was entirely his choice. Whatever happens in his life is absolutely none of my business. Yet, despite this I feel an unwelcome and nagging urge to reach out and contact him. Being cold and despondent just isn't me, but there is no way of getting in contact without risking him finding out about the baby.

I consider for a short time if that would be such a bad thing after all, it would certainly be a weight off. Keeping secrets is an exhausting business and I am in a constant state of anxiety that I will somehow be discovered. The only way he might find out about the baby is if my Dad were to give in and tell him, but I trust Dad not to betray me, even though he thinks I am doing the wrong thing.

I decide not to call him back and delete the message. Later that evening as the baby and I are settling into bed, my phone rings. Matthew again. I let it go to voicemail, but this time I listen to the message straight away.

"Hey Tess, it's Matthew. Listen, I'm concerned about you and I just wanted to check that you are ok. No-one from work has heard from you in a long time and your Dad won't tell me where...err how you are. Just send me a message when you get a chance and let me know you are ok? Thanks. Bye." He sounds genuinely concerned and I feel bad to be stonewalling him. Would it hurt to ping him across a message just to let him know I am ok? Maybe he does care about me after all. That is a nice thought, but I try to ignore it. I type out a quick text message to let him know I am ok and then turn my mobile off and try to get some sleep.

CHAPTER THIRTEEN

I've picked the perfect day to visit the graveyard. The sun is bright in a baby blue sky, but the air is still positively Baltic. The baby looks quite ridiculous, swaddled to the point she can barely move any of her limbs, just a tiny pink face peeking out from a white snowsuit. She seems fairly happy though, as I push the pram along the boundary of Morn Hill cemetery. I visit often. It's become a morbid tradition, like visiting grandma in the old people's home. This time is different though. I have questions to ask, but no-one is there to answer them. It might seem like a pointless exercise, but what else can I do?

Throughout my life I have always held this image of my mother in my mind, formed from snippets of photographs and scraps of conversations, all collaged together to create an entirely fictional person. On the rare occasion that people would speak about her in front of me, I would cling on to every last word, squirreling them away in a strongbox in my head, taking them out at night to form a fantasy Frankenstein of the woman who once walked the earth and held me in her arms. As a small child I would often sit cross legged on the floor in the lounge, poring through photo albums, stroking the wrinkled pictures, trying to get a sense of this person who loomed large in my life despite being entirely absent from it. To me she has always been tall, beautiful and demure. Eminently sensible and clever; in short nothing like me.

The paint of her portrait in my head is cracking and peeling away. The ghost I grew up with fading, like a character in a fairy-tale as it ebbs from your memory as you grow older. Yet, it strikes me that my father has always worshipped this person above all others. I don't recall a single occasion he has ever said anything bad about her, certainly not in my presence and yet she abandoned him too. Why was he not angry and bitter? Perhaps she was worth the pain. At least he had some comforting memories to cling onto. All I had was weary photographs and other people's memories.

Her grave is immaculate. I know this before I even arrive. My Dad visits once a week, every week without fail. Her headstone is gleaming and glossy in the winter sun. The grass is neatly clipped up to edge, where her neighbours sprout messily, abundant with weeds. A small pot overflows with lilac roses and lisianthus, wilting in the frosty air. I reach out to touch the stone, a ritual I have developed, as if I am touching her in a greeting.

"Hi Mum." I say. I used to feel self-conscious about talking to her grave, although it was something that Dad had always done. As an adult it seemed a bit nuts; whatever had been physically here of my mother was now long gone, but the more I visited the more I realised that everyone seemed to do this when visiting the grave of a loved one. Either way, it made me feel better than if I had just sat in silence.

"So, Dad had some interesting news for me." I'm trying not to sound angry, but I do feel angry. "He told me what really happened to you. That you left us. I'd like to think I can understand why you did what you did. Apparently, you were unwell and couldn't take it any longer. I know how that feels. I feel it every day.

You see the problem for me, is that I have always looked up to you. I know that's odd considering I never really met you. But all through my life, when I've had to make difficult decisions or I've been struggling I would think to myself, what can I do that would make my Mum proud. If she is sat up in her cloud in heaven, watching over me, what would she want me to do. And I had always thought you would be gunning for me, but now I am wondering.

We spend our lives, watching films where the hero fights and survives and then they all live happily ever after. Did you actually fight? Or did you just give up as soon as things got tough? Honestly, I want to know. How much did you really suffer, Mum? Because I have been suffering all of my life, because of the way that you chose to end yours and the only silver lining that I had was this image of you as this perfect wonderful person. You weren't though. You were selfish and weak." I was crying.

"The only thing that I have learnt from you, is that sometimes there is no happy ending. Sometimes, people just die, and they leave nothing behind, no happy memories or benevolent legacy. They just die and then they rot in the ground until they are completely forgotten. I'm your legacy and just look at the state of me."

I could say more but the venom has exhausted me. I sit cross legged on the cold, damp floor by my mother's grave, picking at the grass. As the anger has ebbed away, I feel I am left with a void and I simply don't know what to do with myself. I look up at the pram, which stands a few feet away. She is quiet but I don't know if she is sleeping or listening to my insane rambling. It doesn't really matter. I won't be bringing her here again. I won't ever be coming back here. I've wasted enough time mourning the ghost of a woman who never existed.

I'm waiting for the tears to stop falling and building up the energy to haul myself off the ground when a Robin flutters across the grave and lands on the pram. She is small and impossibly delicate, claws gripped on the edge of the pram hood. She shakes herself and puffs up her feathers. She is beautiful. As I watch her, I realise she is watching me with her little dark eyes. I move to stand up but she doesn't even flinch. As I approach the pram, she watches me but doesn't move. I look into the pram to see the baby is wide awake and watching the small bird who is peeking over into the pram. I slowly reach out my hand, am amazed when she allows me to gently stoke a finger down her back. She is tiny and soft. She opens her beak and sings bold notes, before flying deftly away. I wipe away the last of my tears and push the pram out of the graveyard.

My Nan, Ivy, lives a ten-minute drive away from the graveyard, a journey she often walks to visit her daughter's grave. Her house sits alone, by the side of the road leading into the city, half way down the hill and it looks almost as small and ancient as she does. The wall to the garden and a small outbuilding which was once the only toilet, are crumbled over and the paint of the windows is curled and flaked. It is haloed by the sight of the grand cathedral in the distance at the centre of Winchester; a view that is still breathtaking to me.

I park around the corner, on double yellow lines as there is literally nowhere else to park, praying I don't get caught by one of the city's many overzealous parking inspectors and carry the baby to the front door. Flakes of paint burrow under my fingernails as I grasp the door knockers and tap it gently.

"Just a minute." Nanna calls and we stand waiting for an eternity while she shuffles to the door. When it finally opens, I could swear the old lady has shrunk. She peers up at me with her ancient, watery eyes, which are incongruous against her current outfit of luminous yellow lyra leggings and a mauve fleece. She looks like an extremely dynamic person, who just happens to be moving in slow motion.

"Tess, my flower! Come on in maid." She ushers me in through a narrow hallway into a bright beige lounge at the back of the house. Once I'm seated in front of the noisy convection heater she has been nursing, Nanna bustles around me to gather up the bits and pieces required for company. By the time she has appeared back with a teapot and plate of biscuits, I have managed to peel myself and the baby out of our coats.

"Oh my, and this is this my little great-granddaughter!" She says, finally sitting in the chair opposite me. The house is incredibly hot, we are practically sat on top of the fire. "May I?" she holds out shaking arms for the baby. I gratefully place the baby in Nanna's arms and set about making the tea, lifting up the tea pot lid I'm not surprised to find just the one teabag between the two of us. Nanna is brimming with pride and she nags me to take a picture for her. She inexplicably has the latest iPhone, which is surely down to my Dad. Always happy to share his wealth, particularly if it gives him an excuse to buy yet more tech. "Do it on my mobile flower, then I can show the girls at my dance club. I can't believe I'm a Great Grandmother. I'm far too young!"

she flashes a wicked smile, and something causes her to pause and regard me a little closer.

"Before you say it, I'm fine. Just tired." My stock response was wearing thin.

"You look like you've been crying." Nanna looks worried. She's not one to beat around the bush and she's certainly not about to be fobbed off by my usual "I'm just tired" nonsense.

"Dad came around this morning with Aunt Sophie."

"Oh yes."

"Apparently they decided that now was the time to tell me how Mum really died." Nanna flinches. I forget sometimes that I am not the only one that was affected by my mother's death. Now I know the truth about how she really died, I finally understand why they have all been so reticent to talk about her. It must have hurt the people who knew her and loved her, more than I could ever imagine. Suddenly I feel like an imposter, with no right to mourn my own mother, after all I had never really known her.

"Oh dear."

"I don't really know what to do with this information, to be honest." I sit back in the chair, exhausted and close my eyes.

"You mustn't be angry with her you know." She says very quietly.

"Really, why not?" my voice is rising, "And if not her then who should I be angry with? Dad for letting her do it or you for not being supportive enough?"

"Now you stop that Tess! That is not fair!" She is still a formidable woman, despite being only four foot five and the tone of her voice stops me. "It was nobody's fault and you mustn't think like that. Would you get angry at someone with cancer for dying? No, you wouldn't. It's much the same thing. She was very unwell. She had struggled with depression all of her life and we all did what we could to try and help her. When you were born, we thought that would be the end of it. She was so smitten and desperately in love with you. She put on a good show too; everyone needed to see how well she was coping. Some things never change really. Motherhood always has been one big competition. It's silly really. Anyway, in the end it seems, she just thought you would be better off without her."

"How ridiculous. And selfish and stupid." I mutter.

"It may seem ridiculous to you dear, but to her it was everything. She wanted the best for you and the way I see it, she thought she would only harm you. As if she might infect you with her depression, it is a disease after all, no less deadly than cancer."

"I'm sorry Nanna, I didn't mean to be so..." she held up her hand.

"Don't worry about it my flower. I don't know what Sophie and your father were thinking telling you this now."

"Perhaps they think I'm not coping?"

"Are you?" she asks.

"I don't know." I say.

Later that night I lay awake, staring at the ceiling and considering my future; it makes for a bleak landscape. Broke, alone after eighteen years of servitude to a tyrant of a husband. My mood is the darkest I can remember it ever being and I just don't feel myself. Granted I've never been a little ray of sunshine, but this grim depression is the worst I have experienced so far. It seems easier to imagine the world without me in it. The people I love, simply carrying on their lives as if I had never existed. I feel certain that the baby would have a better future without me. I am, after all, a terrible mother. Just like my own. Maybe it is genetic?

People die every day in accidents, just suddenly snuffed out, disappearing like a wisp of smoke. Most of them wake up in the morning, oblivious to their fate; a sudden heart attack, a fatal car crash or they simply fall asleep and never wake up again. It seems cruel, there are those of us that would be willing, grateful even, to submit to oblivion, while others happily going about their contented lives should have it snatched from them against their will. Where is the justice in that?

I wish I could choose my fate – a more honourable departure. No slashed wrists or dismembered body parts littering the train tracks, or bloated bodies being fished out of the lake for me. A packed funeral service full of sorrow and mourning rather than a handful of shell-shocked souls, struggling to make sense of the end I have chosen. While my heart is aching for them and their pain, while I consider most carefully my own fate, I struggle to find a better way forward.

Sadness engulfs me suddenly and without warning I am wracked with huge pitiful sobs that slip unnoticed into the darkness. I clasp a hand over my mouth to try and quell them, so as not to wake the baby. If this is the end, I have chosen for myself, then why am I so sad about it? Can I be brave enough to consider the alternative: carry on living with this pain? Carry on suffering every day? And if so, for whom am I doing this?

Tears drench my cheeks, but I can feel exhaustion creep up. I'm bored of this melancholy. I just want to fall asleep and never wake up.

CHAPTER FOURTEEN

When the healthcare visitor arrives the next morning, the condition of the house has slipped back somewhat and the baby and I are still in our jim-jams, having forgotten completely about her visit. Thankfully she is unlikely to make it as far as the kitchen where dirty dishes are, yet again piled up in the sink, a full bin bag is sat by the backdoor waiting to be transferred into the wheelie bin and the bin itself is so full the lid can no longer be closed. As long as I manage to keep her in the lounge, she would be unlikely to get a whiff of the several days' worth of nappy sacks. When I open the door at two in the afternoon, I am greeted by Polly, who explains she is new and taking us over. She is a short woman with a kind, lined face and immaculately styled short blond hair, I initially warm to her and we effortlessly enter the routine of tea bringing and baby weighing.

When she has finished her checks, she sits back in the armchair, picking up her cup of tea for the first time and looking at me in a way that makes me feel instantly on edge.

"So, do we have a name for the baby yet?" she says with a smile that looks forced to me.

"Err...no. I just, I haven't had the time or headspace." I reply with a smile that I hope achieves a little more authenticity than hers had.

"Well, legally you have to register the birth within 42 days, just to make you aware." She says this as she scribbles copious notes on a file. I watch her intently, hoping her face will give me some kind of clue as to what she is writing. "So, you do still have stacks of time. Do you have a list of possibilities?"

"No." I say, caught slightly off guard and then I panic. "I was thinking maybe..." I look frantically around the room...lamp, sofa, green carpet, books, aha...Tess of the D'Urbervilles! "Tess?" Crap. I'm an idiot.

"Oh..." I see her eyes flick to the top of the paperwork to double check, yes Tess is also my name. She appears to be thinking furiously of an appropriate response. I'm cringing. "That's a lovely name. Any other options?" she fires back. Frantically scanning my cosseted book collection, I am distracted momentarily and briefly consider naming my daughter after the mouse in my favourite book of all time.

"Algernon." I am fairly certain Algernon is a boy's name. Today is not going well.

"Alrighty then," says Polly, "and are you still breastfeeding?"

"No. I really did try but my milk just dried up and she was so hungry all the time." I'm desperately trying to justify myself but as I ramble and she is scribbling frantic notes, I'm starting to feel a simmering panic bubble up through my chest.

"I'm sorry to hear that," she says finally looking up, "I'm sure you tried your best." Her smile seemed condescending and I resent being made to feel like I have failed. I just shrug, hoping the less that I say the sooner she will bugger off. "And how are you feeling? In yourself?"

Her question knocks me off guard somewhat. I guess I feel like any mum of a newborn; bewildered, exhausted and fed up. If I come back with a twee, everything's roses and honey blossom type answer, I am fairly certain this shrewd old thing will see straight through me. I decide to settle for a semi-honest response with a hint of nonchalance.

"I'm ok I guess," I say with a shrug, "just tired." She nods and writes some more notes.

"Do you mind me asking how things are with the father of the baby?" she asks. Why the hell these women think that was any of their business infuriates me. Were there not millions of women in this world who cope caring for a newborn without a man in their life? Did they think that I was particularly inept and would fail immediately at motherhood without a partner by my side? I bite back a barbed, sarcastic response whilst attempting to explain the very basics of my situation, not offering any more information than I really have to. Polly nods and attempts what seems to be a look of sympathy, but actually looks like pity. There's a subtle difference.

She drains the remainder of her cup and I make to get up and see her out, but she continues to write her notes, so I sit awkwardly watching her in silence. Meanwhile, the baby who had been happily lying on the floor on her play mat starts to grumble. I ignore her, but as the silence draws on, I see Polly look up from her paperwork, first to the baby and then to me. Taking my cue, I drop down onto the floor on my knees and lift the baby from the mat. I know she isn't hungry, so I give her bottom a cursory sniff. All is well in bottoms-ville so I place her back down. Her grumbles amplify immediately. Feeling the gaze of "Polly The Judgemental" upon me I sit back up on the sofa, with the baby snuggled in my arms. The grumbles continue as she squirms and kicks out her legs. Feeling my face redden, I watch her helplessly for a moment, not sure what to do next. Just in case, I fetch a bottle from the kitchen, hastily warmed in a cup of boiling water and offer the teat to her. She pushes it away with her chubby little hands and starts to cry. Oh God, not now, I think.

"I'm sorry," I say to Polly, "she's not normally like this." Polly looks unfazed.

"Has she been teething recently? It's a bit early but it might be that." She suggests and I'm comforted by the realisation Polly seems to be as clueless as me.

"No, I don't think so," I say, my voice is trembling. This is a disaster. My vision blurs with tears. I feel the sofa beside me dip as Polly sits down, her hand gently rubs my back.

"It's ok, nothing to worry about. Try giving her the knuckle of your finger to chew on." I bend my index finger and the baby pulls it eagerly into her mouth. Her gums are solid as she grinds them against my finger. "You'll need to get some teething gel from the pharmacy and maybe some teething rings to put in the fridge. Ah look, she's a bit happier now." I can't see as my eyes are full of tears that I am desperately fighting to hold back. Polly gives me one last pat and then retreats to the armchair. I can hear the scratch of her biro against paper. Another damning report of my ineptitude from the Healthcare professionals. Just what I needed. I wipe away the tears with my spare hand.

"Sorry," I say with a great snotty sniff, "I'm just tired."

"It's ok. Really." Polly doesn't even look up at me. "It's incredibly difficult when the baby is this young. More so if you haven't got any support to help you out. Really, you shouldn't feel bad." Feel bad that I'm doing a dreadful job I think as I fight back a sob. Great, just the encouragement that I need. Thanks Polly. "Do you have anyone supporting you at the moment?"

"I have some friends locally and my Dad isn't far away." She nods and she scribbles.

"That's good. Anyone else?" she asks.

"No." I reply, my voice quivering.

"Do you feel like you would like some extra support?" she asks.

"Like what kind of support?" my voice rises in irritation. Why is she implying that I need help? The baby was well fed and looked after, what more does she want?

"For example, someone to talk to about how you're feeling?" How the fuck would that help exactly Polly, I think. What I really need is a full night's sleep, a bucket of gin, about half a million pounds and an orgasm would be nice.

"No. Oh No. I'm fine. Just tired." I say, again. I'm getting sick of hearing myself say it. She nods again and stares at me. I hold her stare, hoping she will feel uncomfortable and leave. Instead, she reaches into her bag and pulls out some leaflets.

"Well, I'm just going to leave these here for you," she places them on the table. I angle my head to read the covers. One is about NHS services for new mums, another is about breastfeeding and the last one is about Post Natal Depression. I glare at her, but she is too busy packing away her things. Finally, she stands, shrugs on her coat and walks to the door. Before she turns to leave, she hands me a small dog-eared card.

"If you need any help, or even if you just want to talk, give me a call. My personal mobile is on there, so you can call any time of day or night, ok?" she places her hand on my arm in a gentle gesture. I avoid looking at her, instead studying the card intently.

"Thanks, see you next week." I close the door as she walks down the path. Then I scrunch up the card and throw it across the room. I am furious that I have let her see me cry. So far that is a hobby I reserve for when I am lying alone in my bed at night. God only knows what she is thinking of me. Judging by the leaflets I have been left, she thinks I am about to lose my marbles, if I haven't already. I am not entirely convinced that she is wrong, either.

The day is slipping into darkness by the time I have dressed myself and the baby. As we walk down to the pharmacy, she fusses quietly in the pram while my sleep deprived brain wonders idly if Algernon really is such a ridiculous name after all? It certainly has a ring to it. When we arrive at the pharmacy, I ask the young blond counter assistant (who is in my opinion wearing enough make up for two people) for some teething gel. While she is fetching it from the shelf behind her, I enquire casually whether she knows if Algernon can be a girl's name. She confesses that she isn't sure and looks at me in the most peculiar way while I pay. I rip the box open immediately and rub the clear gel into the baby's red, hot gums.

"Aww...she's cute." The girl behind the counter says. I tense dreading the next question "What's she called?"

"Algernon." I reply, noticing with satisfaction that the baby is starting to settle. Not noticing the reaction of the girl, I turn the pram and head out of the chemist.

As we walk home, darkness is clambering in and the bright Christmas lights along the high street twinkle against the blackening sky. I watch the baby's tiny face, eyes wide as she is mesmerised by the spectacle. I look forward to a time when we can walk hand in hand admiring the pretty displays, or decorate our own little Christmas tree, although in my imagination we aren't in our snug little cottage in Grove road, we are somewhere larger and more homely. A proper family home.

We arrive back at the house, just as a red-faced delivery man is trying to manoeuvre his large van in a 3 point turn in the narrow street. Realising with a start, this is my weekly food shop, I hurry into the house, parking the pram in the dining room, thankful that the baby has taken this opportunity to have a snooze. By the time he reaches the door, the delivery driver is in a foul mood and dumps the plastic bags onto the doorstep for me to ferry across to the kitchen. The last item, which hadn't fitted in one of his little plastic crates is a small artificial Christmas tree with a plastic box of gold and red decorations. It was the cheapest that I could find and ordering online didn't require balancing it on the back of the buggy as I struggled to get it home from the shops.

Once the shopping is packed away and the baby has been fed and changed, I prop her up in her corner cushion, so that she can watch me from the sofa as I struggle to assemble the little tree. It is a far cry for the enormous real trees Matthew and I had always bought to fill up the living room in the old house, but in line with the old tradition and for my own comfort, I have set a fire going and put the TV onto one of the music channels so the house is filled with a bit of Christmas cheer. Algernon (as I am currently referring to her, until I have decided on a slightly less ridiculous name), watches with curiosity as the lights flash and the sparkling baubles are hung, and then re-positioned and then re-positioned again. When I've finished, I turn off the light and we sit in the warm glow of the fire, comforted by the twinkling tree lights and snooze together.

When I wake, I realise several hours must have passed as the fire had fizzled down to glowing embers and the TV has long since gone onto standby. The lights from the tree still sparkle, but ever paranoid of setting off a house fire, I clamber off the sofa to turn them off, placing Alergnon on her corner cushion as remarkably she hasn't woken. The room plunges into darkness and having left the warmth of the blanket I shiver. Hugging myself, feeling suddenly very awake I pull on a cardigan, which had been left on the back of the arm chair. It does little to keep out the icy chill of the night. Shuffling carefully into the dining room I switch on the light, wincing at its brightness, and look at my watch. It is past midnight. This must be the longest stint of undisturbed sleep I've had since she was been born. Great work Algernon, I think with a smile. I turn to walk into the kitchen, as I haven't eaten all day and I'm starving. A noise from the lounge stops me.

Ding...ding...ding...

I pause, my groggy brain struggling to make sense of the sound. It continues as I walk back into the living room and then stops. Careful not to wake Algernon, I turn on lamp in the corner of the room and look around. A small movement by the Christmas tree catches my eye and I move closer. On one of the lower branches, a string of wooden bells painted bright red, quivers slightly and then stops completely. Puzzled, I prod the largest bell with my index finger. Ding...ding...ding. It swings slowly with the momentum. It is definitely the noise that I heard, but I can't fathom how it had made that noise by itself. I stand and watch the tree for a moment, hoping for a clue and then I turn.

She is stood in the doorway; a hunched up black figure. I can't see her face, just the whites of her eyes as she glares at me. I scream.

CHAPTER FIFTEEN

A fist hammers against my door. I barely hear it over the Algernon, who is howling in my ear. The letterbox flaps open and I hear Tom's voice.

"Tess! Are you alright?" he shouts. I open the door and he rushes in, materialising like a superhero out of the darkness of the night. Relief crashes through me. Although I haven't known him very long, I just feel safe when he is around. The oppressive atmosphere of the house vanishes in a heartbeat. "I heard a scream, are you ok?" his handsome face is scrunched up in a concerned frown.

"I'm fine...I think." My voice is quivering again but I don't want to cry again today. It has been a long time since I felt like someone cared about me. "I thought I saw someone in the house..." The words were barely out when Tom charges past me, into the kitchen. I hear him mutter "Jesus Christ" as the light flashes on in the kitchen and he comes face to face with the scene of utter devastation.

"I think you've been robbed." He calls to me. Sheepishly I join him.

"Yeah...no...it was like that already." I flash an awkward smile. He grimaces and flicks off the light.

"There. That's better" he says with a grin. Then he runs off up the stairs. I hear footsteps charging from room to room (all two of them), while I silently pray, I haven't left any greying underwear lying around. I reason this is unlikely, as I haven't actually changed my underwear for three days. Most of it is piled up in front of the washing machine.

He reappears looking slightly flushed.

"There's no-one here." He says.

"I didn't think there would be."

"What? I thought you said..." My face flushes in embarrassment. What I was about to say seemed suddenly very foolish to me.

"I thought I saw her..."

"Who?" he looks confused and adorable. Adorably confused.

"Mary."

"What the... Mary Donoghue? The baby-murdering wench of Grove Road? I hate to break this to you Tess, but she's dead. I reckon for the past oooo, let me see, one hundred years or so! I'm so sorry for your loss." He was laughing now.

"I know this sounds crazy, but I saw an old woman dressed in black stood just there." I point to the doorway, which happens to be where Tom is standing and watch him shiver and jump away from the space, "Then she just disappeared."

"Ok and just how much wine have you had to drink this evening?" he says, in an admonishing tone that is not at all serious. It strikes me that his crooked grin is rather sexy, and I feel myself blushing hard.

"How very dare you!" I laugh, "I haven't touched a drop in months!"

"Well this is probably as good a time as any to start."

"I'm afraid I don't have any alcohol in the house at all." I say.

"A-ha! Because you've already drunk it all! You dirty old lush!" we both grin. "I might just have a bottle or two next door, would you care to share a nightcap with me?"

"I think I am going to need it"

"Nice tree by the way," he says as he rushes out of the door to fetch the wine. I place Algernon in her moses basket as she has settled nicely back to sleep and I fetch a couple of glasses, stopping to check my reflection in the bathroom mirror on the way back. My hair isn't too atrocious considering it hasn't been washed today, but my skin looks almost a grey colour. It isn't a great look, so I hastily brushed on some blusher and squirt some deodorant, before heading back to the lounge, realising I have left the wine glasses on the toilet. I hurry back to retrieve them and then place them down on the side table in the lounge. I'm just flicking the Christmas lights back on as Tom arrives back in a desperate attempt to chase away the eeriness of my encounter and soften the lighting to a more flattering hue.

"Nice." He says as he closes the door behind him and for a second I think he is talking about me "Cosy...I like it." Maybe not.

"Thank you," I say, glad of the dim light in the room as I'm sure my cheeks are colouring just because he is gloriously handsome and in the same room as me. We sit on the floor, with the baby's basket between us, warming our backs against the radiator. I sense that we were both in need of a bit of comfort and company.

"So, tell me about this ghostly apparition." He nudges me in the side and holds out his glass so we can chink.

"Well, she was dressed all in black. Her dress had one of those huge bustling skirts, it just looked Victorian to me. And then she disappeared."

"Oh, I thought you were going to say it was just a black shape and then I was going to say, there's nothing to worry about it was just corner of the eye phenomenon. You know, where you catch something in the corner of your eye and your brain fills in the gaps."

"I'd rather that explanation than accepting that my house is haunted by an evil old woman who has been dead for a century."

"Okay, let's go with that then," he smiles in an attempt to reassure me and it almost works. "Your brain is generally much more receptive to these kinds of events when you are tired or run down. How have you been feeling?" He studies me and I decided it is futile to lie. Even the best blusher in the world couldn't hide the state of my face.

"I'm exhausted and I haven't been eating, which probably doesn't help. Oh, and I'm hormonal and emotional, which I understand is very normal." He nods.

"Yes, that's perfectly normal. Along with random crying episodes, shouting fits, bouts of extreme grumpiness and a tendency towards casual alcoholism."

"Are you some kind of parenting expert or a doctor?

You seem to know a lot about this stuff?" I've been dying to ask him what he does for a living since we'd bumped into each other at the library. It's not the kind of place you expect to bump into dishy men.

"Nope. I'm the CEO of a national charity promoting literacy in children." I struggle to respond as that is nowhere near what I had been expecting.

"Wow, that sounds very impressive." I manage finally.

"It's pretty demanding but I love it. What do you do? When you're not being an exhausted mum that is?" I'm surprised he has asked and not just assumed I had morphed into a career-less Mum the moment a baby fell out of me.

"I am a Chartered Accountant. I used to work for the same firm as my ex-husband, but I...err... got fired."

"While you were pregnant?" he looks aghast, "Can they even do that? Did you speak to a solicitor? Or ACAS?"

"Err...no. I was fired for attempting to inflict actual bodily harm on my ex on work premises. Apparently, I'm "very lucky" he didn't press charges." I have the good grace to look abashed at my confession, but Tom is just laughing.

"Fiesty! I like it. Also, I imagine he deserved it?" We nod at each other seriously in agreement. "So, what are you going to do now? I can check if we have any vacancies in our finance department if you like?" I consider it for a moment but sense a danger to our blossoming friendship of introducing a work relationship. Besides, I've tried working with a partner and it reeked of putting your all your eggs in one basket.

"Actually, I think I would like to try something new." I am thinking out loud as this is genuinely the first time, I have felt capable of thinking past the next feed or change or nap. It feels right though, accountancy is killing my brain, and this is a new opportunity to try my hand at something else. But as soon as I have this epiphany, reality strikes, and I realise working with a young child is going to be a challenge but training for an entirely new career would be practically impossible. The wind drops out of my sails.

"Sounds cool, what did you have in mind?"

"I have no idea." I say suddenly feeling quite sad and unfeasibly tired at the same time. My eyelids feel like lead weights and I fight off a yawn, unsuccessfully.

"You best get off to bed." Tom says, "Do you want me to stay over? On the couch I mean. Just in case you have any more ghostly visions ", his words are teasing but I can tell he believes me. For the first time in a long time, I feel like I have someone truly on my side. I want him to stay.

"No, it's fine." I say. "I've got your number if anything else happens. Although, I'm so tired now I think I'd probably sleep right through it." I grin at him sleepily.

"Well, if you're sure?" he stands and then holds out a hand to pull me up.

"Thank you, I'm sure we'll be fine." I stand up with some effort despite his help, enjoying the warmth of his big strong hand gripped around mine.

"Ok, well I'll check on you in the morning if that's ok?" he leans on the doorframe and we look at each other in comfortable silence, which, had there not been a newborn baby sleeping behind us, I think might have been filled with a delicate goodnight kiss. He smiles one last time and disappears into the night.

Cold air billows into the space where he had been and decimates the warmth his presence had brought in an instant. Reluctantly I look to the doorway where she had appeared, but there is nothing there. I pick up Algernon's basket and slowly amble up the stairs to bed. The alarm clock next to my bed declares that it is two am in an angry red display. I grunt and place the moses basket on the bed, before crawling under the covers myself. I sit up and look at my baby, her porcelain face serene and stroke her cheek with my little finger.

"Night, night Algernon" I say softly, "I will think of a better name for you in the morning, I promise."

Tucked up in the covers, it takes what seems like hours to get back to sleep. My mind is racing with thoughts of Tom and the gentle promise of a potential relationship, perhaps? I think of Matthew and how he would react to finding out about his baby daughter. I think about my dwindling bank account and the extortionate cost of disposable nappies. Just before I drift into a fitful sleep, I think of a regretful landfill site piled high with nappies, thanks to my daughter's overactive bottom.

That night I dream again. I'd never had such vivid and disturbing dreams as I'd had in those nights following the birth of my daughter. For the most part they are always innocuous enough, but the common theme seems to be forgetting the baby or leaving her somewhere. The worst so far has been going back to the office at my old job, having parked in the grey multi storey car park opposite the office block. I'd skipped into the office without a care in the world, forgetting that I strapped poor Algernon into the car seat and left her there all day. Each time I tried to leave the office, knowing that my baby was suffering and alone in the car, someone had given me something else to do, delaying my return. That was a pretty horrible one, but Sally had reassured me that dreams like that were pretty common for new mothers. It was just a sign of anxiety - all perfectly normal for a mum of a newborn.

My dreams are meandering tonight, but the one just before I wake seems more lucid and realistic to me. I am in my little cottage and I can hear the baby start to cry. My instincts tell me she is hungry, so I flick the switch to turn on the bottle warmer and fetch a fresh bottle from the fridge. As I walk into the lounge, the house seems to shift around me. The walls grow darker and damp stained with age. The room smells musky and acrid wood smoke makes my eyes feel sore. By the fire, which is nothing but a meek glow, a black figure sits in a small wooden chair. She holds Algernon in her arms and as I approach, she holds the baby out to me. I don't look at her face, I just take the swaddled lump and turn away. I want to get away from this woman, her power over me is foreboding, but I sense that, in this dream at least, we are on the same side for some reason. Even still, I don't linger and hurry back into the kitchen, which is now also dark, with a large cast iron range on one side and long table pushed against the far wall. The room is sooty and hot, and I drag my sleeve across my forehead, realising that I too am wearing a long black dress.

Algernon is wriggling and crying out as I place her upon the table. Without a thought for whether she might roll off, I turn to a dresser on my right and pulled open one of the heavy drawers. The light in the room is poor, but I quickly find what I have been looking for. The baby's cries echo around the room and I worry that the neighbours will hear her fuss. Crossing back to the table, I loosen the little white nightgown from around her neck. Holding on to her forehead with one hand, I hold the bread knife in the other and slice into her neck. I wake coated in sweat and terrified.

CHAPTER SIXTEEN

Sleep continues to elude me for the rest of the night, and I sit sentinel over Algernon, bitterly resenting her contented sleepy sighs. Occasionally her soft pink eyelids flutter and she grumbles quietly, but she doesn't wake. The irony of not being able to sleep on the first night that my baby sleeps through is not lost on me. By the time the morning sun had started to creep through the room, I am so tired my eyeballs feel sore and fragile. I lift Algernon out of the moses basket and lay her onto my chest. She kicks her legs frantically and squeals with delight. All I can think about is my nightmare; the vivid sight of the cold knife sawing through my daughter's neck. I need to get out of the house, so I reach for my phone and call Sally.

We are up and ready to leave the house within half an hour, when there is a knock at the door. I can see the tall outline of Tom through the inset glass of the door and I remember his promise to check on us from the night before. My heart is thumping with excitement as I open the door.

"Hey, you ok?" he sounds concerned as he leans against the doorframe and frowns at me.

"I'm fine, just tired." I say, forcing a smile.

"You sure? You look wrecked." My smile fades. I assume any romantic feelings he might have had were surely extinguished on account of my haggard appearance.

"Honestly, I'm fine." My response is spikier than I had intended, and he seems to recoil slightly.

"Okay, well I was thinking...well wondering...if I could take you out for a meal tonight?" I'm still smarting from his insistence that I look dreadful, so I decide to try and keep my distance.

"I can't. Not really, with the little one. I wouldn't be able to find a babysitter." He interrupts me before I can conjure up any more excuses.

"Of course, silly me." I am at once gutted at how quickly he has accepted my rebuttal, but not for long. "Lunch then. I'll take you to The Swan in town. I've just got some stuff to do in town but how about you meet me there at 12.30?" he says this as he backs down the little path, a cheeky grin on his face knowing that I will struggle to argue.

"I don't...wait...Tom!" he is already striding down the road.

"See you at lunch!" he calls over his shoulder. I can't help but smile.

I rush back into the house and quickly shower and change into clean clothes. Feeling buoyed by prospect of my date (if that is what it is) and despite my lack of sleep, I set off across town to Sally's house feeling slightly less grotty. I hadn't realised, now that the days all seemed to blur into one another, that it is Saturday and Sally is distinctly lacking in the energy required to keep her two eldest children in check in a public place, so she has suggested meeting somewhere she could "contain the chaos". It was only a ten-minute walk, but mostly uphill, so by the time I arrive I am unbearably hot in my thick winter coat and worry I might smell a bit funky for my date. Sally's house is a large double fronted Georgian town house, rather callously situated between the kebab shop and the tattoo parlour at the top of town. It is still gorgeously dignified with a large fern garland hung over the door, twinkling intermittently with soft white lights.

When Sally opens the door, she gathers me up in an enthusiastic embrace and steps back to examine me.

"Christ, you look beat. Rough night?" she asks.

"Yep." I don't need to say anymore. She leads me in through the house, encouraging me to leave the now thankfully sleeping baby in the pram and wheel it through to the back of the house, where an immense kitchen, the kind of which you normally see in glossy lifestyle magazines, spills out into the garden. On the left wall, shiny white units and immaculately clean worktops fill the room. Sally sits me on a stool by the island and offers me a coffee, while I gape, open-mouthed at the huge, suspiciously tidy room.

"How's Poppy doing?" I ask as the coffee machine coughs and splutters.

"Yeah, she's fine. Dan's just popped out to pick up some bits and decided to take her with him. He's so sweet. Although, shame he didn't take the other two." She rolls her eyes as the sound of thumping footsteps overhead grows louder and squawks of disagreement can be heard as clearly as if they were all in the room with us. "Keep it down you two!" she yells out the kitchen door, before closing it on the din. "Hooligans!" she rolls her eyes.

"Thanks." I say as she hands me a steaming hot cup of coffee. I hold it eagerly in my hands, inhaling the bitter scent and feeling mildly rejuvenated by the mere presence of caffeine.

"So! Do we have a name yet?" she looks at me with mock sternness.

"Well, kind-of." I say and she looks mildly impressed. "We have an interim name."

"Go on."

"Algernon..."

"That's..."

"I know, it's boy's name."

"I was going to say, that's a bit weird. But also, yeah, that's a boy's name!"

"The new health visitor asked me, and I panicked."

"Oh my God" she says, "You didn't honestly tell a medical health professional that you are naming your baby girl Algernon?" she looks horrified and deeply amused at the same time. I explain my rather unusual inspiration for my daughter's name and hesitation to admit to the Health Care visitor, who I suspected already thought I had lost my marbles, that I hadn't yet formally named my baby. "Oh well that makes perfect sense then." Sally adds.

"Don't judge me!" I laugh, "I'm very, very sleep deprived. I'm in no fit state to be making important life decisions like the name of my child!"

"Clearly not!" Sally mutters into her coffee cup. I decide this is the time to ask her about my disturbing dreams but then hesitate, not sure if it is wise to admit the dreadful images that have been haunting me at night. Sally sees me bite my lip. "Everything ok?" she asks reaching out to stroke my arm. I'm reassured. Sally is on baby number three; she's been through all of this before. She will understand.

"Yeah, I'm just tired." I say. "I had another nightmare last night." In our last coffee meet-up I had shared with her some of the tamer dreams I had been having, where I had left the baby at home and was wondering around town like loon with an empty pram. Sally had reassured me that these dreams were completely normal and went on to tell me some of the odd dreams she had had when her two eldest were born. I hoped she would say the same about my latest nightmare, but it seemed unlikely.

"Really? What did you do this time? Put the baby on eBay?" she smiles. I manage a weak smile, feeling sick to the pit of my stomach very suddenly.

"No, this one was a lot worse." I take a glug of coffee and then blurt it out, "I dreamed I cut my baby's head off with a bread knife." I can't help it, but the tears are streaming by the time I have finished my confession, as if I really have committed this heinous murder. The dream is still raw in my mind and my consciousness is struggling to filter out the difference between what is real and what isn't. It takes me a moment to realise that Sally hasn't responded. I look up at her and see a momentarily reaction of shock crosses her face before she jumps up from the seat beside me. She wraps her arms around me as I sob against her shoulder.

"That sounds like a horrific nightmare." She says quietly, "But you have to remember, it was just a dream." She pulls away and looks into my eyes, holding my head in her hands, she uses her thumbs to wipe away my tears. "Listen, it's ok. We all have crazy dreams after giving birth. Your hormones are all over the place." I nod dumbly.

"I know, it's just, it felt so real. It was horrible. I could feel the warm drops of blood on my face as I was hacking through and I didn't feel a thing. It was like I was cutting up a chicken breast for dinner." As I ramble, I can see the deep concern Sally is feeling, her brow furrowed into deep set lines as she listens intently to me.

"We all have bad dreams, it's nothing to worry about. But..." She is clambering back on the stool whilst avoiding looking at me.

"But what?" I ask.

"If you ever think you might be capable of harming yourself or the baby, you must tell me. Or the midwife." The words peel reluctantly out of her mouth and she regards me carefully. I am too shocked to respond. I had thought Sally was a friend and ally, but I am now wondering if I can trust her after all. Particularly if she thinks I could be capable of harming my own child. She said it herself, it was just a dream, so this reaction seems a little over the top. A little voice in my head proposes that I had made a grave mistake in admitting my dream to her. I try to argue that Sally is my friend and she wouldn't report me to the midwives. After all, it was just a silly dream. It's not like I actually harmed my child. The silence between us grows as I seek a suitably reassuring answer.

"Of course not." I try to reassure her, but Sally's face suggests that I was not being convincing enough. "Genuinely, I have never had thoughts that I would harm myself or my baby." I say firmly, starting to feel irate that my so-called friend could even suggest a thing. Sally gathers me up into another embrace, this time it is unwelcome, but I respond with as much warmth as I can muster.

She sits back down and smiles at me. I know that she is clever enough to have sensed the seismic shift between us and realise that I am now bristling with hostility.

"You still need to think of a name though. Algernon is just ridiculous!" she laughs. I trot out a fake laugh, to keep up the pretence. She seems to be relaxing and I want to give the impression that I have let it go. I haven't. We chat for a little while longer, covering off the standard staples of new mum conversations; sleep, feeds and the colour and consistency of our offspring's bowel movements. As soon as I think I can get away with escaping I make an excuse about feeling utterly wretched and Sally immediately offers to take Algernon for the morning to let me get some rest. I refuse emphatically, attempting to be casual about it. My mind is set; Sally cannot be trusted.

As I push the pram back out into the high street, a figure dressed all in black steps beside me.

"You cannot trust her." Mary whispers into my ear.

"I know." I reply, keeping my head down. I watch her black boots emerge from under her skirts, landing with a heavy thump with each step.

"She will tell them you are a danger to the child. They will take your baby away."

CHAPTER SEVENTEEN

I arrive at The Swan Inn thirty minutes late, Algernon is screeching in her pram and I am hoping that Tom has gotten fed up of waiting for me and left. All my enthusiasm of the morning has vanished, and I have been dreading the lunch date, keen to get home and be alone with my thoughts. Sometimes I just crave solitude. Tom looks up from his phone as we approach. My heart sinks, he is still here, and I feel wretched for having made him wait. He must see the strain on my face as he attempts to disarm me with a charming smile.

"I was beginning to think you were going to stand me up." He says peering into the pram at the red-faced bawling tyrant.

"Sorry, I did try to say I thought it was a bad idea." I am flustered. I can see the other diners staring at me, no doubt thinking what a terrible mother I must be. Angry faces are turned in our direction and openly frowning and tutting. Why on earth did I think I could possibly enjoy a quiet lunch with a friend? I swing the change bag over my shoulder and retreat to the Baby Change, clutching Algernon to my chest

"I'll get you a drink!" Tom calls after me.

Locking the door behind me, I lay the baby down on the change table, tears brimming in my eyes. I can feel my panic rising, as I silently beg her to be quiet. The whole restaurant must be complaining to one another about the wreck of a mum and her brat of a child. Sometimes the anxiety I feel is like a thick, hard ball in my chest and sometimes it feels like an immense weight pressing down on my whole body. Today it is like that, as if I'm trapped under a dense slab of concrete and I cannot escape.

"Please... please be quiet." I beg, but her protests continue. I let out a muted sob, barely able to see what I am doing as I fumble with her bulging nappy. Her bottom is red raw, so I slather her with cream and hastily apply a fresh nappy. She starts to settle a little, but I know she needs a fresh bottle. Somehow, I have to attempt to orchestrate a date with the very lovely Tom, while the screaming hellion of a child runs me ragged. I wash my hands, gather the baby and bag and head back to the table, still feeling hot and flushed.

"I took the liberty of getting some hot water for a bottle. Figured she might need a feed." My tension melts a little and I feel as though I could cry with happiness. "Here do you want me to do it." He holds out his arms to take the baby. I think I might love the very bones of this man. He has sensed that I am at breaking point and in fact all I need is a tiny bit of help. I hand the baby over gratefully, noticing for the first time a glass of white wine set before me.

"Oh!" I hadn't expected to be drinking alcohol, was that allowed when you were in sole charge of a baby. I sneek a look around the room to see if anyone is glaring at me disapprovingly, but I am surprised to find that no-one is taking any notice at all. "Thank you", I murmur as I take a healthy slug of the deliciously cold wine, savouring the burn at the back of my throat before it hits my otherwise empty stomach.

"No problem. Thought you deserved a treat." He says.

"Are you trying to get me drunk?" I blush at the absurdity of my attempt at flirting.

"Yeah, why not?" he grins, splitting his attention between Algernon who is slurping greedily at her bottle and my flushed face as I try to study the menu as nonchalantly as I can.

"Did you manage to get your chores done?" I say and immediately chastise myself for being so dull.

"Yep, just had to pop into the library." Before I could respond the waitress arrives to ask if we were ready to order. She looks in her early twenties, with long brown hair swept back into a perky ponytail. She smiles warmly at Tom, her bright young eyes flashing at him encouragingly. He signals to me to order first and I notice the gleam drop from her smile. She nods curtly as I order my pasta and turns back to Tom without a word.

"I'll have the Steak and Ale pie please." He says not looking up from the menu laid out on the table in front of him.

"Great choice," she grins and scribbles in her notebook, "that's my favourite. Aww she's cute." The waitress bends down to inspect my baby, and I notice her white blouse gapes at the top, giving Tom a direct view of her bra. She lingers, leaning in close to him to stroke Algernon's hand.

"Yeah, she's gorgeous." He says oblivious to the mammary display being put on in his honour. She lingers a little longer, but quickly tires of the lack of attention being paid back to her and flounces off, her pony tail bouncing from side to side as she goes. "I think she's done." Tom says lifting the baby over the table towards me and I dutifully place her on my shoulder for a burping.

"Well this is romantic." I say as Algernon belches into my ear and he laughs.

"I hadn't expected any romantics so not to worry." He says and my heart dips. I've got this completely wrong. Algernon belches loudly over my shoulder again and I reach out for my glass, trying to hide my dismay as I glug down the wine. Why has he invited me out for lunch then? We sit in awkward silence. The restaurant overlooks the High street, where Christmas lights hang from lampposts, buffeted by the wind. Across the road I catch a glimpse of black. Mary is stood watching me. It feels like a warning.

"So, have you got much planned for Christmas?" I ask, tearing my view away from the window and meeting Tom's eye.

"The plan is to spend the day with my ex-wife and our boys." He doesn't sound enthusiastic.

"Won't that be a bit awkward?" I ask slurping down more wine, emptying my glass in the process.

"Nah. We decided to split fairly amicably. You get to the point where you seem to spend most of your time arguing and you just wonder, is this really best for the kids?" I wonder if his idea of "amicable" was the same as Matthew's. "It was Jane that suggested we split in the end. Strange thing was I felt sadder about the fact I didn't feel sad about it being over. Does that make sense?"

"I guess so." I say.

"What happened with you and your ex? If you don't mind me asking?"

"He decided it wasn't working and he left. I found out later he had been having an affair for a while." It's still humiliating to admit it out loud, but since this wasn't a romantic occasion there didn't seem much point trying to hide the truth of the matter.

"Even though you were pregnant?" he looks shocked.

"Actually, he didn't know about the pregnancy." I say, "He actually still doesn't know."

"Shit!" says Matthew spluttering on a mouthful of his beer. I watch his reaction carefully, expecting a reprimand. "Well, I guess, he's the one that did the dirty on you. So, he's foregone his right to be involved."

"He blocked my number after he left, so I couldn't have told him if I wanted to." I add as if it's a reasonable excuse not to tell a man that he has become a father. I don't intend to mention that Matthew has unblocked me and attempted to contact me. Tom's attention is compelling, and I don't want to lose his sympathy.

"Well, there you go then!" he says refilling my glass. He flashes a disarming smile at me, and I let myself relax a little. I glanced out of the window, but Mary has gone. He follows my glance and looks at me quizzically, but I just shrug. Algernon is by now snoozing happily on my shoulder and as I attempt to transfer her into the pram beside me, the perky waitress arrives with our meals. She makes an effort to flash her big blue eyes at Tom as she places his plate in front of him, but he is too busy salivating over his meal. I feel triumphant, although he's not paying that much more attention to me than to her. The steak and ale pie has thus far received the most enthusiastic reaction from Tom.

"Have you seen any more of our friend Mary, by the way?" he says as he shovels a forkful of pie and mash into his mouth. I pick delicately at my pasta, attempting to look demure, although my appetite is nagging at the pit of my stomach.

"No, not since last night."

"Ah, so you do think your house is haunted then?"

"No, I didn't say that!" I protest through a mouthful of food.

"Do you believe in ghosts?" He eyeballs me, curious for my response.

"I don't really know to be honest." I think about it for a moment. It's not something I am keen to accept. The implications are pretty huge. "I guess I would like to think if ghosts really did exist, then my mother would have tried to make contact somehow."

"Oh sorry, I didn't know your mother had passed. What happened?" we are talking freely now, and he doesn't ask if I mind if he asks. I don't.

"Car accident. I was very young. Still a baby." I only realise a moment after I have said it that I have lied. This is the story I have been giving my entire life. It just slipped out, although subconsciously I may have thought better of admitting there is a family history of mental health issues.

"Christ, that's rough." He says and I shrug.

"I've never known any different." I don't want to sound callous, it's just the truth. "My Dad has always been there for me when I needed him, so I genuinely don't feel like I've missed out as such."

"Must've been tough for your Dad?" he asks.

"Yeah, I'm only really beginning to appreciate that actually." I smile and Tom smiles back. "Do you believe, by the way?" He looks confused, "In ghosts." I add.

"Oh! Actually, I do. I will have you know I was Chief Ghost Tour Actor in Lancaster while I was at university."

"Oooo, get you!" I laugh.

"Definitely one of my finest achievements." He sits a little taller and I can tell this is one of his prouder accolades.

"That doesn't necessarily mean you believe in ghosts though."

"I do." he says earnestly. "In all honestly, it's a bit bleak to think that we just die and that's it. Don't you think?"

"Yes, but it is also fairly bleak to think my Mum could've found a way to make contact with me from beyond the grave, but she hasn't." He thinks about this for a moment.

"Maybe she has." He answers finally, "Perhaps not in a full-blown apparition kind of way. Either way, I'm sure she has been watching over you." He says this quietly. We had strayed into very tricky territory for a first date or whatever this is, but I am touched by the sentiment. I sense that he is trying to pep me up.

"Hopefully not all of the time." I say with a crooked grin. "That would be very weird." Tom laughs.

"Yep, good point. I'm pretty sure she would be really proud of you right now, doing all this by yourself."

"I'm not sure about that." I say grimly, "I'm not doing very good a job!"

"Nonsense. You're doing a fantastic job. Don't forget I have done this, twice, as part of a couple and we struggled. I think you are coping brilliantly." I try to fight back the tears pricking at my eyes.

"Thank you. It's kind of you to say so, but it really doesn't feel like it at the moment." I shovel some more pasta into my mouth to try and hide the fact my bottom lip is quivering.

"I think you are doing a great job. If I'm honest, I'm slightly in awe of how you are coping." I study him to try and decipher if he is being disingenuous. He seems to be pretty earnest, but I doubt myself.

"Thank you." I mutter again, trying to convince myself to believe and trust him. I look up and a black shape catches my eye. Mary is brooding across the road again. Her stare is unwavering and unsettling. I can tell she is unhappy.

CHAPTER EIGHTEEN

Back at the house, not even the cheerful lights on the Christmas Tree nor the gentle warmth of the fire can comfort me. Algernon, sleeps contentedly, swaddled in a colourful fleece blanket and propped up in her corner cushion beside me. I watch her face, the little rosebud mouth pinched in an unfeasibly serious expression for a two-week old baby. She frowns and then smiles as the gas noisily escapes her nappy. I slip my finger into her hand and she grips it gently. She feels deliciously warm and soft and I wonder to myself if I really could live without her in my life. Mary assures me that I can. She says that my life would be easier and better if I entrusted my baby to her care. She urges me to handover the noisy little tyrant. It's not that easy I say to the empty room. It is true that I have become rather attached to the little girl and even now I am fighting the urge to pick her up and hold her warm little body against mine so that we can sleep happily together. Just me and Algernon versus the world.

My phone buzzes loudly as it vibrates against the hard wood of the side table. I look over and see Dad Mob on the screen. I ignore it. That is the thirteenth time he has tried to call me today. I've no idea what he wants but I'm not in the mood for talking to anyone today. When I look back to my baby her eyes are open, and she is looking at me. I'm not sure how much her little eyes can focus on, but I'm sure that she knows who I am. I move closer and smile, before placing a gentle kiss on the tip of her nose. She grabs at my hair with her hands and when I pull my head back, I see she has clung on to a few rogue strands. Her eyes are dark blue and wide as she takes in my face. Her hands are clenched tight and she kicks out her legs. We just look at each other, me smiling, her staring in wonder. And then, very slowly, the tiniest smile tinges her lips. I wait for the normal violet expulsion of gas from her bottom, but it doesn't come. She is actually smiling at me. I grin and pluck her off her cushion holding her against me, tenderly stroking the back of her head with my hand, savouring the soft warmth of her cheek against mine. My heart feels full; full of her. My beautiful daughter Algernon (I really need to come up with a better name). I look to Mary, who has been regarding this scene from the other side of the room. She tells me that I need to take urgent action if I want my daughter to stay with me. I nod. I know what I have to do.

There is a bang at my door and Mary disappears. The fist bashes against it twice more urgently. I'm taken by surprise and freeze staring at the door until I hear his voice.

"Tess..." he shouts, "Tess! I know you're in there." I jump up with the baby in my arms, hurrying through to the dining room, where her car seat has been pushed under the table. I pull it out and settle Algernon in. She looks alarmed and I shush her, placing a quick kiss on her cheek before rushing back to the front door, which I have no intention of opening. I am standing to one side of it, when the letterbox swings open. "Tess!" he shouts again and lets it clang shut. I'm pressed against the wall to the side of the door, my heart thundering in my chest and at a complete loss as to what to do. To my right, I see a shadow at the window. I'm hidden by the thick curtains which run from the ceiling to the floor and the Christmas tree beside me. I cannot see Matthew but from the shadows thrown on the opposite wall I'm guessing he is peering through, trying to see into the hallway. I realise he will see that the fire is lit and the Christmas tree lights are on and so he will know that I am home.

The shadow disappears and the letterbox flaps opens again.

"Please Tess. I just want to talk to you." He sounds a little calmer, but I don't budge. "Listen, I know things didn't end well between us and that I've not been in touch, but I really think we need to talk." Why now, I think, and how the hell did he find me? Suddenly the calls from my Dad make sense, and I accept there is yet another person I cannot trust. Why do people keep doing this to me?

"Please open the door. It's really bloody cold out here." I sink to the floor and cross my legs. There is absolutely no way I am ever letting that man back into my life. I wonder if my father has told him about the baby too. The betrayal stings.

"Tess...I know about the baby." He speaks calmly through the letterbox. My panic is rising. What does he want? Is he here to take her away from me? He had always been as keen to have a baby as I had been, and the miscarriages had taken their toll on him as much as on me. Afterwards he seemed to drift away. I understand now why he was so desperate to escape our doomed marriage. Staying with me meant accepting that he would never be a father, while Suzy offered a better option. But I had seen them together in the baby shop and I had seen clear signs of a blossoming baby bump. Perhaps Suzy had lost her baby? Or perhaps there had never been a baby and now Matthew was reaching out in desperation to me. If he was looking for sympathy he had come to the wrong place.

In the silence my mind races forward. If Suzy failed to produce offspring for whatever reason and then he had found out about my baby, was he now trying to win me back? It seemed unlikely, and so I jump to the only other conclusion. He is here to take my baby away from me, so he and Suzy can raise her as their own.

"C'mon Tess, this is ridiculous. Please...just open the door and talk to me like a sensible adult." He is no longer talking through the letterbox. I hear him rest his back against the door with a thump and now he is just shouting at me through the door. After a few more moments of silence, I hear his fist thump against the door.

"For fucks sake, Tess! It's my child. I have a right to see it." Angry Matthew is more familiar to me than calm Matthew. I continue to do what I always did when he was in one of his rages. I keep quiet and don't move. Better to let him get it out of his system than try to diffuse him. In the other room I can hear Algernon start to whimper. The letterbox flips open eagerly. He is straining to hear the baby's cries.

"Please, I just want to meet my baby." His voice sounds quiet, pleading and ultimately pathetic. Not a chance in hell, I think. Algernon's cries get louder and more urgent. I'm not sure how long I can keep this up, she needs a feed and I can't bear the thought of her hungry and distressed. I wonder if I can sneak across the room back to the dining room without him seeing me. Clearly, he knows I am there, but somehow it seems important he doesn't see me. As if I have held up a cloak of invisibility to our lives and while he has found our house, he hasn't really found us until he physically sees us.

It is so cold out there and I think of him shivering on the ice-cold stone doorstep. Happy memories of the man I used to love, perhaps still did, resurface uninvited. I imagine tears slipping down his soft, clean shaven face. Despite all he has taken from me, I still care for him. What's the worst that can happen, I wonder. He can't just rush in and take her from me, can he? I have the power to give him what he has yearned for all these years, in a moment, and it makes me feel cruel to withhold it from him. I stand and reach for the door.

"No..." whispers Mary's voice in my ear and I hesitate. "He will take her from you."

"I'm going to speak to my solicitor" Matthew practically spits the words through the letterbox, "and I am going to get access to my child." The letterbox claps shut, and I hear Matthew's angry footsteps thump away from the house. Algernon's wails have amplified again, and I hurry through to the dining room to sweep her up in my arms.

"It's ok," I whisper kissing her head, "The horrible man is gone now." After fixing her bottle, we sit on the floor in the dining room as I feed her. I am on edge, expecting Matthew to reappear at any moment. I try to think, but my mind is a whirl of panic. In my infinite wisdom I have paid a full year's rent up front. Clearly, I hadn't banked on Matthew tracking us down. My mind races through where I might go; there is only one plausible choice but there is no way I am running back to my Dad's again. Especially after he has betrayed me like this. Perhaps this is what he had been planning. Panic rushes up my throat. I am trapped.

The room grows cold and dark, as though a thick black cloud had blocked out the sun.

"I can help." says Mary. She is stood in the doorway to the kitchen. "I'll make sure no-one ever takes your baby away from you."

"How?" I plead and she tells me what we are going to do.

CHAPTER NINETEEN

It is the day before Christmas Eve. I used to call it Christmas Eve Eve, back when I had a sense of humour, but only because I knew that the silliness of it would annoy Matthew. Algernon and I are lying on my bed cuddling. I've spent most of the day dangling colourful plastic toys over her, encouraging her to reach up and grab them and then letting her pull them into her eager mouth. I realise with a pang that I could do nothing but this all day long, but Algernon is growing tired. Her eyelids are dropping, and she quickly settles into a snooze. My own eyes feel heavy, but I cannot sleep. My stomach is growling too. I haven't eaten at all today and I don't particularly want to, which is just as well because the kitchen is devoid of food besides powdered formula milk.

My phone has finally stopped ringing. I suspect that this is because the battery is dead. Either way, it is still downstairs in the lounge and I have no intention of going to fetch it. I wonder idly who is trying to contact me and what they want. Most likely it's nothing good. Perhaps it was Matthew's solicitor or the midwife, or even my father insisting again that I come over to his for Christmas Day. We're perfectly happy in our little bolt-hole. I've wrapped a couple of the toys that Dad and Aunt Sophie brought round and placed them under the tree. I know it's a bit cheap, but I'm certain than Algernon won't be any the wiser and I simply cannot afford to be wasting money on any more toys, she has plenty.

I haven't heard from Tom since our lunch date yesterday. I haven't seen him come or go from his house, so I think he's either dead or ignoring me. It occurs to me that I could simply text him and see if he wants to come around for a cup of tea, but then again, if he wanted to, he would have been in touch surely? I wonder if this is another friendship that I should write off and it feels like a safety net had been pulled out from under me. Our friendship had been tenuous and new, but I still felt curiously safe with him, in a way I had never felt with Matthew. Perhaps we were meant to be together? I'd probably never find out now. It feels as though I have scared him off forever.

The air in the house feels dense and claustrophobic, but we cannot leave. Mary tells me we are safe while we are here, and I trust her. As it grows dark, I brave moving us downstairs, casting a nervous glance outside before pulling the curtains in the lounge tightly shut. I light a fire and turn on the tv. The silence is starting to drive me nuts. The bright flashing lights of the screen captivate Algernon, as they do me, providing a brief respite from the relentlessness of my busy mind. I need to find a safe place for us, I think. I've already told you what to do, says Mary. I know, but isn't there another way, I ask. No, she says. Maybe tomorrow, I think, and Mary goes silent. I worry that I have upset her and lost my last ally. I allow myself to be swept away by the tv for a bit of peace.

Afternoon TV is festively dreary, but my brain is grateful for the respite. I sit through a feature about the best starters to serve your guests for your Christmas Eve party and wonder idly when that became a "thing". For me Christmas has always been about family, the rest of the world ceases to exist for a few short days. This year family is just me and Algernon (I really must come up with a better name; the clock is ticking). I try to convince myself that I wouldn't have it any other way, but the truth is I feel bereft of the company of my dad and Aunt Sophie, and even Matthew. This year would be different; dark, quiet and lonely. The TV host has moved onto a feature about top tips to keep the needles from falling off your tree; I've not registered a single word she has said.

There's a knock at the door and I'm instantly on edge. I listen carefully, expecting to fall under siege from my ex-husband. Silence and then another light knock. I creep to the window to peek through the curtains. I'm surprised to see the light of the day has almost completely faded. The small figure of the Healthcare Visitor is standing at my door. Mary tells me to ignore her. Whatever you do don't answer the door, she says. It doesn't feel right to leave her out in the cold, so I open the door and force a smile. Polly looks apologetic and apprehensive.

"Hi Tess," she says "I'm so sorry to do this to you at short notice. I know we're not due another visit until tomorrow, but I wondered if we could get it done today? I just happened to be in the area and with it being Christmas Eve tomorrow, well, I'm sure you've got better things to be doing!"

"Of course." I say ushering her in. She smiles gratefully and places down her bags and weighing scales before shrugging out of her heavy winter coat. Her blue linen dress looks flimsily inadequate. She shivers.

"Gosh it's bitter out there," she says, "they're saying it's going to snow later today. Another good reason to get all my visits over and done with today!" She laughs but I can see her watching me carefully. I offer to get her a cup of tea and she eagerly accepts, kneeling down to lay out her scales and pull out her paperwork. I try to listen out for her from the kitchen, but the kettle is too loud, and Mary is whispering at me to hurry up. When I plonk down the cup of desperately anaemic tea for Polly, she looks at it without enthusiasm and takes a tentative sip, trying to hide her grimace.

"So, do you have much planned for Christmas?" I ask her and she seems surprised by the question.

"Oh, just the usual. The kids have been back from uni for over a week, making the house look untidy. Oh, to be a student again!" I smile and consider that would actually be really nice. A chance to start over and make a better job of things. "How about you?" She watches me eagerly and I know I have to answer carefully.

"I thought we would just enjoy our first Christmas together, just the two of us." Polly nods thoughtfully and I suspect this was the wrong answer. As if to make the point, I kneel beside Algernon and pick her up gently, making a show of stroking the back of her head and kissing her cheek. I bring her closer to where the midwife has set up her equipment and place her on the floor to undress her ready for weighing. To my relief, her nappy is dry and clean.

"And, do we have a name for the little one yet?" I can tell Polly has been keen to ask this question since she arrived. I curse myself, knowing I should have prepared for this. My mind has been such a jumble I cannot seem to process the most basic tasks. The fact I have only had about five hours sleep in the past three days is not helping. I pick up my cup of coffee, taking a slow slurp to give me time to think.

"Not yet." I say and register her disapproving look. "How's she doing?" I ask before she can admonish me.

"Good. Very good weight gain this week. She's doing really well." Polly looks up at me and regards my face for a moment. My stomach choses this moment to rumble loudly, "How's mum doing? You're looking a little bit pale. Are you looking after yourself ok?" My mind freefalls into panic. My face must betray me as the look of concern on Polly's face deepens.

"Oh! I'm fine!" I try to laugh it off, "Just a bit tired and I'm trying to lose some of the baby weight." She doesn't look convinced. In fact, she looks me up and down and I become aware of the fact my maternity jeans are hanging loosely around my waist.

"I didn't see you at the mother and baby group this week, are you still meeting up with Sally?" I wonder how she knew that I had been meeting up with Sally and then I realise, this isn't a last-minute call by to clear her Christmas Eve for tomorrow. Sally must have called her and told her about the dream. She is here to check up on me.

"Yes, we're still meeting up. I saw her yesterday actually." I say in a matter of fact tone that I hope will settle the issue. I don't mention that I have no intention of meeting up with her again.

"That's good. So, you're not spending Christmas with any family?" she asks. I'm getting irritated. We've already been over this. Surely, I can't be the only single mum spending Christmas home alone with my child.

"No. Just me and Al... the baby." I flush deep red. Shit. Polly just smiles.

"Who is Al?" she asks. None of your sodding

business, I think.

"No-one. Sorry, I'm just tired." I force a yawn. She's staring at me with an intensity that I do not like. Then she turns to scribble notes in her book. My heart is thumping in my chest.

"Ok, well if you need anything at all or would like to talk to me over the Christmas period, you have my number. Actually, I'll just write it down here for you again." She scribbles it onto the front page of the red book and hands it to me. I take it and place it on the arm of the sofa without looking at it.

"There's really no need. We're absolutely fine." I manage a smile that I'm pretty sure shows every single tooth in my mouth. Polly looks dubious. She's onto you, Mary whispers from the door. I look to her and try to shush her. When I look back at Polly, she is looking at the empty doorway, her brow furrowed in confusion. She looks back to me and we regard each other in silence.

"Can I just pop to your loo?" she asks, "Too much tea!"

This is your chance, whispers Mary.

"Of course." I say directing her across the hallway. I have Algernon in my arms. As soon as I hear the door lock click into place. I rush to the front door and run out into the cold night air.

CHAPTER TWENTY

Got to get away. They think I'm going mad, but I'm not. We hurry through the streets, Mary leading the way. Barefoot in the snow, carrying a baby that is naked but for her flimsy nappy, I'm sure people are looking at me, judging me. Everywhere I look I see hostile faces. I don't know where we are going. Mary has promised we will be safe, but most importantly together. Got to get away. I'm sure that woman is just steps behind me, and I look back. I cannot see her. She must have ducked out of view.

I'm out of breath. The baby is trembling in my arms. Oh God, why is this happening to me? I cannot cope. I am not ok. Everything around me is a dark blur, except the shadowy form of Mary ahead of me. She is beckoning me down a dark alleyway. This is the way to the lake. She tells me it is the only way, so I follow. I check behind me again but cannot see anyone. I'm certain Polly has called the police. Got to get away. I cannot cope. I am not ok.

I can't stand it anymore. I can't just sleepwalk into them taking her away from me. I have to do something. Otherwise they will take her away and give her to Matthew and Suzy. Although I'm sure they would make better parents than I would. Perhaps she would be better off with them. Mary hisses at me as I hesitate in the dark alleyway. No, I cannot let this happen. She belongs with me. I know how it feels to grow up without your mother and I won't let that happen to my baby. I won't let them take her away. Got to get away.

I feel dizzy, so I lean against the wall and crane my neck up to the sky. The air is so cold I feel like the tears will freeze on my cheeks. A billion tiny snowflakes hurtle down from the sky onto my head. It looks so beautiful I gasp, and the cold air hurts my lungs. Mary is cursing me in whispery tones but I'm too captivated to move. She reminds me they are coming for me and my baby. I am not ok. I am not ok. I am not ok.

A tiny Robin hurries across the sky and lands on the window ledge above me. She has her head cocked so that she can see me better. I watch her as she fluffs up her cherry red breast against the chilly air and takes a few tentative hops along the window sill, before flapping down and landing on the ground in front of me. I bend down and realise just how tiny she is. Her black eyes never leave mine. I can sense Mary moving in the shadows, but I cannot take my eyes from this brave little creature. It hops a few steps closer and I stretch out my hand. She flutters her wings again and hops onto my knee. I'm shocked at first, feeling her little claws digging into my jeans, her weight almost imperceptible. I crook my finger and gently stroke across her back. The little Robin closes its eyes as if my touch is bringing it comfort.

Mary is looming over me now, but the little bird doesn't fly away. It remains defiant on my knee. I can feel the anger seeping out of the shadow beside me, but I am so mesmerised by the friendly little creature that I cannot move. The shadow of Mary lashes out suddenly and the Robin takes flights in fear. I look into Mary's snarling face. Silly little woman, she hisses grabbing my hand and squeezing it hard enough to hurt, don't you know what they will do if they find you? I take a reluctant step towards Mary, when a door opens into the alleyway. I'm blinded by the light from within the building and I hear a familiar voice say my name.

CHAPTER TWENTY-ONE

"Tess?" Tom is standing in the door. I cannot see his face for the brightness behind him, but I recognise his deep, soft voice. He approaches me and slides an arm around me, gently guiding me inside and as I look back Mary is scowling at me from the shadows of the alleyway. I look around me, we are in a restaurant. I recognise it as the place he took me to on our lunch date, except we have entered through the side door from the Inn's car park. He ushers me into a spot beside the fireplace and places his coat around my shoulders. He pulls off his jumper, his tee-shirt riding up as he does so revealing his midriff, which I'm desperate to touch. Laying the jumper out on the table, he takes the baby from my arms and lays her in the middle, swaddling her tenderly before handing her back to me. I envelope her in a protective embrace and place a soft kiss on her cold cheek. She is shivering so hard her bottom lip is quivering.

  The world is coming back into focus and I see people at the bar have turned to look at us. I look down at the tiny baby in my arms, her face is pale, but her shivering is subsiding. What have I done? What was I going to do?

  "What's going on Tess?" Tom asks as he sits beside me, his arm is wrapped around my shoulders and he pulls me against his warm body. I wonder if I can possibly tell him that I was on my way to the lake, where I intended to drown myself and my baby.

  "I'm not okay." is all I can manage before the tears start to fall. He says nothing and holds me a little tighter. I focus on a Christmas tree, twinkling gently in the corner of the inn. It is hung with old fashioned wooden decorations and golden angel's hair. The warmth from the fire is intoxicating. I realise I have been shivering uncontrollably and draw in a deep shaky breath, releasing it slowly and feeling my panic ebb as the air flows out of my lungs.

I want to tell Tom everything, just to get all the thoughts and worries out of my head. I look up at his face, he is watching me closely, concern etched within his frown. He brings up his hand to softly stroke my cheek and places a soft kiss on my forehead. I realise I am safe.

"I've been feeling...really down..." it's a hard thing to admit and if I'd said it to anyone-else I would have felt like I'd made myself irreparably vulnerable. He doesn't say anything, just nods. "I don't think I've really felt myself since she was born. I'm struggling Tom." The tears come then so violently. He squeezes me harder, neither of us caring about the people around us. When I finally started to calm, he raises my face to his.

"Where were you going?" he asks. For a while I can't answer. The words choke in my throat.

"The Lake." I say finally. When I look him in the eyes, I realise he understands and, in that moment, I could love him forever for the simple fact he hasn't made me say it out loud. He knows and he's still here, holding me tight.

"Let's get you home and then we can get you some help, okay?" I nod. He releases his hold on us and reaches under the table, fumbling momentarily and then handing me his boots. "They're about ten sizes too big but they should stop you from getting frostbite on your feet." I managed to lash the laces around my ankles to stop them falling off and we step out into the night.

The town is alight with festive lights, hung between the buildings on either side of the high street and draping from streetlights. It's beautiful. Algernon cranes her head back to get a better view of the sparkles and flakes, her deep blue eyes wide with wonder. On the opposite side of the street a large nativity scene had been set up in a small wooden shack, with a collection box for the local church. I clomp the heavy boots across the road.

Hay has been scattered across the floor, where

models of cows and sheep kneel, faces turned down respectfully. The three wise men stand in the background, their gifts held out and heads bowed reverently. Joseph stands behind where Mary is sat, the bundle of Jesus held tight in her arms. I study her face, a mask of serenity, the faintest hint of a smile on her lips. She looks at peace, calm and happy. I consider it is not an entirely accurate representation of the glorious post childbirth scene for a first-time mum, but that doesn't really matter. At the back of the scene, in twinkling fairy lights is one word; hope.

"Um...I should probably mention, I ran out on the Healthcare Visitor. She's still at my house." Tom is shivering beside me, in a t-shirt and jeans. I'm fairly sure the icy coldness is seeping through his thick woolen socks too.

"We'd better get a move on then." He says and we walk back to the house. I keep looking around for Mary, but she is gone.

When we arrive back at the cottage, Polly is leaning in the doorway, looking out into the darkness frowning. She spots us as we turn the corner and gasps.

"Where have you been?!" she cries. She clocks the tear streaked redness of my face and hustles me into the house. Tom walks in behind us. He is now shaking uncontrollably.

"I'll make us a cup of tea." He manages to say through chattering teeth. I sit on the sofa, the baby still swaddled close to me and Polly sits opposite.

"I'd like to go through a questionnaire with you now Tess. If you don't mind?" She says the words softly and I nod. She picks up her folder and a pen. "Okay, have you found that you have little pleasure or interest in doing things?"

"Yes"

"How often? Some days, more than half the days or every day?"

"Every day." She makes a note.

"Okay next, have you found yourself feeling down, depressed or hopeless? Again, if yes, how often" She looks up at me after reading out each question. She no longer seems judgmental to me, just concerned.

"Yes, Every day." I say.

"Have you had trouble falling or staying asleep, or

sleeping too much?"

"I was having trouble with sleeping too much, but now I'm hardly sleeping at all. I keep having really vivid, horrible nightmares." She jots down some more notes.

"Ok, we'll come back to that... Have you been feeling tired or had little energy?" she continues.

"Yes, both, every day."

"And how has your appetite been? I have to say you look like you have lost a bit of weight."

"I'm hardly eating at all. I don't have any appetite, except for coffee." I smile miserably and then sniff back some snot.

"Have you felt that you're a failure or let yourself or your family down?" she looks up at me then in time to see the tears filing up my eyes. I nod slowly.

"Every second of every day." My voice is barely a whisper. At that moment Tom appears in the doorway, three mugs in his hands which he places on the side table. He kneels at my feet. I pull up my sleeve to wipe away the deluge of tears.

"You're not a failure and you haven't let anyone down." He says firmly and gently kisses me on my forehead. I lean forward and rest my wet face against his strong shoulder. He holds me there while I sob. I feel Polly's hand on my back, rubbing up and down. I feel myself start to calm and sit back, tears still falling and snot streaming down my face.

"Have you had trouble concentrating on things, like watching the tv or reading?" Polly continues.

"Yes." I answer with a sniff. Tom disappears into the bathroom and reappears with an entire toilet roll, handing it to me before sitting beside me. I unravel several pieces and blow my nose noisily. It takes several attempts to clear all of the gunk.

"Have you been moving or speaking slowly, or been very fidgety, so that other people could notice?" I shook my head.

"I don't think so" I murmur.

"Ok, this last one's a toughie. You okay?" she looks at me and I nod. "Okay. Have you thought that you'd be better off dead or of hurting yourself in some way?" She doesn't need me to answer as I sob loudly. Tom pulls me close to him, rubbing my arm protectively. "I'm sorry Tess, but I have to ask, what thoughts have you been having? Have you thought about how you might harm yourself?" It takes a long time before I can compose myself enough to answer. Each time I open my mouth to respond, a fresh sob escapes. Polly waits patiently, smiling at me reassuringly and placing her hand on mine and rubbing it gently.

"Are you going to take Hope away?" I finally manage to ask.

"Hope?" Polly asks.

"I've decided to call her Hope."

"That's a beautiful name." Tom mutters in my ear and Polly smiles broadly at me.

"That is absolutely the last thing we want to do Tess. But I do need you to answer the question. I'm sorry. I know it's hard." I explain to her then that I had intended to take my baby to the lake and drown us both. Polly and Tom listen carefully without speaking.

"Ok," Polly says, "I would like to get you some help, if you'll let me?" I nod. "Can I ask first, have you been having any hallucinations, as in seeing or hearing things that aren't there?" Her question stops me dead. Very slowly I nod my head. "Can you tell me about it Tess?" she asks.

"I think...I thought...my house was haunted. I found out that a woman who lived here years ago, did terrible things. She murdered children, lots of them. I keep thinking I've seen her. Sometimes she talks to me and tells me to do things."

"Was it her idea to go to the lake?" Polly asks.

"Yes." I wonder if Mary is still here and listening to my betrayal.

"Tess, I think you may be suffering from a condition known as Post-partum psychosis, it is fairly rare and really quite serious. I think a lot of the symptoms that you are experiencing fit with this condition. I need to get you to speak to a GP, today if possible." As she explains her diagnosis panic starts to rise in my throat, this was more serious than even I had thought.

"Are you going to take my baby away?" I ask again, my voice shaking with panic.

"No. Absolutely not." She says, "But I need to get you to a doctor straight away." She fumbles in her bag for her mobile and walks out into the dining room to make a call. I turn to look at Tom.

"Have I done the right thing?"

"Yes. Without a doubt." He says and we both slump back on the sofa. Hope is still wrapped snugly in his jumper, slumbering peacefully. We sit, watching her contented snores. "I think you're very brave." I turn to look at Tom and our eyes meet. Despite the fact I am fairly sure I looked a complete state, I lean in and place a soft kiss on his lips. His hand reaches up and weaving his fingers through my hair he pulls me in a little closer. In the midst of this tender moment, I sniff loudly and feel his mouth curve into a smile. When Polly bustles back into the room, we lurch apart like guilty teenagers.

"The surgery has a GP who can see you right now." she says, and I peel myself off the seat. I place Hope on the floor to unswaddle her from Tom's jumper and she grumps as I dress her in a clean babygrow and then wrestle her into her fluffiest pramsuit. I hand Tom back his coat, jumper and boots, before climbing into my own winter coat. Tom insists on driving me down to the surgery and I appreciate him offering to be there with me. I suspect the appointment with the doctor, might be equally galling but I feel better for knowing I have already confessed my sins and the consequences haven't been what I had expected. If I'd known all I had to do was ask for help, I could have saved myself a lot of heartache and pain.

We park at the little surgery, perched on the very edge of the town. Most of the lights in the building appear to be off suggesting they are closing up for the evening. The receptionist is winding a thick scarf around her neck as we walk through the automatic door and she signals at a door to our left, which stands open. A doctor appears. He is wearing a bright red jumper with a picture of a reindeer on it. There are bells attached to the antlers and Hope is jiggling excitedly as he makes his noisy approach. I shake his hand and notice that he appears to be about twelve years old. When he smiles though, I see reassuring little wrinkles at the edges of his kind blue eyes. Leaving Tom in the empty reception, I walk into the doctor's office, Hope's car seat looped over my arm.

We both sit and I notice the room is icily cold. The temperature is dropping steadily, and the doctor rubs his hands together. My eyes are fixed on the corner of the room over his shoulder, where a black shadow is growing. He follows my gaze, but apparently cannot see the black figure materialising in front of me. Mary is snarling at me.

CHAPTER TWENTY-TWO

The doctor quickly realises something is wrong. He stands to take my arms and urges me to look at him. His voice is soft and as I listen to his words, I feel able to peel my eyes away from the apparition in the corner.

"It's ok," he says, "take a deep breath." I do as I'm told, shutting my eyes to focus as the air gushes in and out of my lungs. When I open them again, the figure is still there, but she looks blurred around the edges.

"I'm sorry." I mutter, burying my head in my hands. I'm too exhausted to even cry anymore.

"I've spoken with Polly," he says sitting back down and scooting his chair around so he is facing me, "I believe that she is concerned that you might be suffering from Postpartum Psychosis, but I would like to run through the questionnaire with you again, please." I nod. He takes me through similar, but not quite the same questions as Polly had, his frown deepening with every answer that I give. Each time I respond, I look up to the corner and find that the image of Mary had dissipated a little more, until it is just a small, black smudge. I can no longer feel the vehemence of her presence. When the doctor asks me about hallucinations, I tense again.

"I've been seeing a ghost of this woman in my house." I answer. I'm pretty sure that if he doesn't already think I'm nuts he will now. Even I'm convinced at this stage that I've gone crazy.

"Not so unusual I guess," his response surprises me, "if you do have a haunted house." He's smiling at me now and we both relax a little. "But seriously, we have to assume that your house is not haunted and therefore these are hallucinations. Now, tell me about your current state of mind. Do you think that you could potentially harm yourself or your child?"

"I don't. Not anymore." I say eagerly, "but I have felt that way. I feel a lot calmer now."

"Ok. Normally what I would like to do in this circumstance is to find you a placement in a specialist Mother and Baby Unit. To be clear, you would not have your baby taken away, but you would receive the support you need to help you through the issues that you have been having. However, before you arrived, I called all of the units in this county and the next and they are all full. God bless the Tories and their unholy austerity measures." He says before muttering bastards under his breath and scooting his chair around to face the computer. "So, the first thing I am going to do is give you a prescription for Anti-psychotics, which should help with the hallucinations that you have been experiencing and also a course of anti-depressants. Unfortunately, these will take some time to work, so I need to know that you have a strong support network around you. I understand from Jen that you currently live by yourself?" He turned to face me giving me an intentionally stern look over his glasses.

"Umm...yes."

"I'm not comfortable with you being by yourself. Is there someone you can stay with who can support you?" I think for a second. There is really only one place.

"I could stay with my Dad."

"Ok, that sounds better. I would like to speak with him before I am happy to release you though, just so he is aware of the support that you will need. Otherwise, get these prescriptions sorted today and I will want to see you the day after Boxing Day to check how you are getting on. In the meantime, I will let you know if a place comes up in one of the Mother and Baby Units and I will arrange for Polly to check in on you regularly at your father's house. Does that sound like a plan?" I nod. Was it really that simple? I scribble down my father's telephone number, which he exchanges for the two prescription notes and I go out to reception. Tom looks up eagerly.

"How'd it go?" he asks.

"Okay, I think. I'm not being shipped off to the funny farm. Well not yet anyway." I smile to show him I'm only joking. He takes the baby seat off me with one arm and wraps the other around me in a comforting hug.

"Yeah, they don't do that anymore. All the funny farms got shut down years ago. You're not going home, though are you?"

"Nope, looks like I'm spending Christmas with my Dad." I say feeling childishly excited by the prospect. The thought of being home alone had been a particularly dreary one, but it was my self-imposed punishment. Whereas, retreating to the relative safety and cosiness of my father's home feels like a huge burden has been lifted from my shoulders.

"Perfect!" says Tom, "And I will be at the end of the phone whenever you need me. In fact, my ex only lives ten minutes down the road from Winchester, so we could even meet up for a cheeky drink now you've got childcare sorted!" he says with a cheeky grin.

"I would say that's inadvisable..." says Dr Hughes, who has appeared behind us. "Sorry, but you cannot drink alcohol on this medication."

"That's fine," I say, "I'm not that bothered."

"Brilliant, you can be my taxi driver. I'm going to need a stiff drink or six after Christmas with my ex-wife" Tom adds cheerfully.

"Your Dad is on his way to pick you up. Have a nice Christmas and see you on the twenty-seventh." I thank Dr Hughes and he shuffles back into his office. Tom drives me to the late-night pharmacist at the other end of town and sits in the car with Hope while I dash in. The counter assistant's eyes flash up to my face when she reads the scraps of paper and I blush.

"These will just be a minute." She says pleasantly as she hands them through a cubby hole to the pharmacist. She rings up the bill on the till and I realise that I will need to get a job very soon if I am going to be able to afford to stay on this medication for the long term. When the paper package is handed back through the hole, I clutch it to my chest and walk back out to the car, all the while resisting the temptation to scrabble open the package and neck a couple of the pills straight away. The doctor had said it would take some time for it to start working and somehow, that meant a delay of even a few minutes was unacceptable. I decide to wait until we get back to the house.

Tom's little blue hatchback pulls up alongside the curb outside his house and mine. I look up at the front window of the house and mentally remind myself; it's not real, she's not there. I turn to him.

"Would you mind coming in with me?"

"Of course. Would you also like me to call for an exorcist while you are away?" he adds looking deadly serious, but I assume he must be joking.

"Would you?" I grin back at him, "Although I think the church generally frowns on that kind of thing these days."

"My Mum has a friend, she's a mystic, type psychic sort of thing. She's called Jenny. Last name Taylor." He giggles in a way that is somehow boyish and charming at the same time. I frown.

"Jenny Taylor?" I say and crack up laughing. It feels good to be laughing.

"Seriously though, she's into all that kind of stuff. Do you want me to get her in to cleanse the house?" he made the quote marks with his fingers for the word cleanse.

"Don't suppose it would do any harm." I say. "Thank you. For everything you've done today. I really, honestly, appreciate it." I turn to face him. He is staring at me with a serious look and concerned eyes.

"Don't mention it." He leans forward and we meet with a tender kiss. "If there is anything you need while you're away...anything at all...just call me. I'll be there in a flash." He brushes a stray hair out of my face and strokes his thumb down my cheek. I don't want to get out of the car, into that cold foreboding house. I just wanted to stay in the warm little car with him.

"I will," I say, "I promise."

"Come on you. Your Dad will be here soon, and you need to get packed." I groan and peel myself away from him, flinging open the car door. Tom comes into the house and we both stand apprehensively in the lounge for a moment, listening. The house is silent, so we shrug at each other and Tom settles to make a fuss of Hope while I crash around gathering clothes and nappies and bottles. By the time Dad arrives I have amassed, one small bag of Christmas presents, one small bag of clothes for me and several large overflowing bags for tiny Hope.

Having introduced them, Tom slinks off happy to leave me in my Dad's care.

"Good grief! How much crap does one little person need?" Dad says as he attempts to carry all of our bags at the same time back to the car, before returning for the pram and then the moses basket, huffing with the effort. After much swearing and rearranging he manages to fit everything into the estate's voluminous boot and returns to the house to wrap me in the kind of aching bear hug that only a concerned father can give. "Let's get you home" he says.

The drive back to his house is slow and laborious due to the thickening snowfall, but it gives us time to talk properly. There are things that need to be said about my mother's past and there are things he needs to know about my current condition.

"You're staying with me until you feel 100%. No arguments." He says looking sternly over to me.

"Yes Dad." I answer like a petulant teenager, although I am secretly delighted to feel at last like some of the pressure is being taken off of me.

"By the way, your Aunt Sophie is going to be staying with us for Christmas too."

"How about Nan? Will she be there too?" I ask.

"No, apparently she's taking a cruise around the Mediterranean with some of her friends from her dance class."

"Won't it be a bit cold?"

"No idea, but she seems pretty happy to be away. I think when you get to her age, Christmas rather loses its shine. Old girl gets rattier and more bad tempered every year. Anyway, Brenda will be with us too. Her and Sophie are ridiculously excited about having time with the baby."

"Oh, by the way, I've come up with a name at last.

I've decided to call her Hope."

"Hope." He says quietly to himself and then smiles. "That's a very pretty name. I like it."

"Me too." I say smiling at him. For the first time in months I feel truly calm and at peace. We sit in silence for a short time, while I decide whether to ask my next question.

"Dad?"

"Yes."

"Why did you tell Matthew about the baby?" I ask looking at him.

"I didn't. He already knew." He says, "He told me his sister had been out shopping in Alton and had seen you in town with a pram. Apparently, she managed to follow you back to the house. He rang me a few days ago to shout at me because he couldn't get you to answer your phone. I tried to get hold of you to warn you, but you weren't answering for me either. I got in a bit of a state actually. I have to confess, I called the local health authority to try and get hold of your midwife. Just to check you were ok."

"Ahh" I say, "that answers a lot of questions."

"Did he manage to get hold of you?" he asks gingerly.

"No," I say, "Do you think we should invite him round to meet Hope? Tomorrow maybe?"

"I think that would be a lovely idea." I can hear the relief in his voice, and I set about texting Matthew the invitation.

"Don't mention that I've been ill, though will you?" Although I was feeling better, the niggling threat of him taking my baby, when he'd helped himself to so much of what was mine already, wouldn't go away.

"Absolutely not." Dad says firmly, "Don't see how it's any of his business. I still think he's a sniveling little prick, but he should still be able to meet his own daughter." I laugh and my phone jumps alive with Matthew's lightning quick response.

CHAPTER TWENTY-THREE

Seeing Aunt Sophie for the first time, knowing that she is aware I have been suicidal, is horrific. I feel as though I have callously dragged up all the pain and hurt of losing her sister, but my trepidation is unfounded. As soon as the car pulls up outside the house, she bounces down the stone stairs from the front door and takes me in a warm embrace, before snatching the baby seat off me and dashing back into the house to introduce Brenda to the newest family member. Dad and I unpack the vast contents of the car into the hallway and I sneak a peek around the door of the living room. Standing proud in the centre of a large bay window, a magnificent real Christmas tree stands twinkling in the dark, two dozen or so brightly wrapped presents stacked neatly around its base. I've come home.

I follow Dad to the back of the house, where Aunt Sophie is cuddling Hope, while Brenda hovers over her shoulder, cooing. Hope is awake and stares up at her Great Aunt with big excited eyes. As Aunt Sophie goes in for a big soppy kiss, Hope breaks into a huge gummy smile and everyone says aww.

"We have a name too." Dad says proudly. Everyone looks at me expectantly.

"Hope." I said unravelling my scarf and pulling up a chair at the table. Brenda and Aunt Sophie approve heartily.

"I can write a name on her presents at last!" exclaims Brenda hurrying down the corridor. Dad shrugs out of his coat and excuses himself to try and shift some of the bags up into my room. The room falls silent as I watch Aunt Sophie, who is clutching my baby, staring down at her in matronly rapture.

"I'm so sorry." I say in a quiet voice. Her head snaps up at me.

"Oh nonsense!" she says, perhaps more loudly than she had intended, startling the baby. "You have nothing to be sorry for at all. Don't you dare apologise. We're just so glad we can help you. In the way we couldn't help your Mum" her voice was cracking but she tried to keep it steady. I move seats so that I am sat next to her and put an arm around her shoulders. Resting my forehead against hers, we both sit and look down on little Hope, attempting to swallow down our grief. "You're so much like her." Aunt Sophie says eventually.

"Am I?" I wasn't too sure I knew much about her at all. Everyone had always found it hard to talk about her and I had learned at an early age not to ask too many questions for fear of upsetting them.

"Oh gosh yes. Stubborn little thing she was too. Although, we had absolutely no idea she was struggling. Well, there was no such thing as post-natal depression back in those days. People talked about the Baby Blues, but generally they didn't think too much of it. Women were told to just pull themselves together and crack on." She sighs sadly.

"Sounds pretty tough." I say.

"It was." She is starting to get agitated, "You know hardly anyone came to your mother's funeral?" I am shocked.

"Why not?"

"They thought she was selfish and horrid for leaving her baby like that. Absolutely no sympathy whatsoever for how she was suffering. No compassion for the illness that was torturing her every single day. Bastards! The lot of them! Your parents were very well connected back then; they had a huge group of friends. Practically none of them showed up. I don't think your father has ever been in contact with them again."

"Oh, I just assumed that Dad was a bit introverted like me." I say. I sense I should be infuriated for my Mother at the harsh treatment by her so-called friends, but I decide that they don't sound like the kind of people who are worth the time and energy of getting angry over.

"He has become more so since your mother died.

Besides, raising you by himself, he didn't really have time for a social life. I don't think he minded though. He'd much rather of spent time with you love." She was calming now. I found it hard to imagine my Dad's life before I was born. Being forced to be both Mum and Dad seemed to have been all consuming and his entire life seemed to revolve around parental duties until I had left home.

Aunt Sophie and I sit in amicable silence until the distinct rumble that I have come to associate with a rapidly filling nappy greets us along with the unmistakable smell that usually accompanies it.

"Ah, I'll leave this one for you, shall I?" I say with a cheeky grin. Holding the baby at arm's length, Aunt Sophie hurries down the corridor.

"Incoming!" she yells, and Brenda and Dad quickly appeared to come to her aid. I wander into the lounge and watch, out of smelling distance, as the three of them battle to change the tiny nappy and dispose of the waste, without any spillage on my father's rather expensive beige carpet. It is all going swimmingly until Brenda, who had been charged with disposing of the offending item in a nappy sack, realises she has a smear of yellow poo on her hand and runs screeching to the kitchen to wash it off. I sit on one of the large lumpy sofas, my feet rested on a large pouf, laughing at the shenanigans. Eventually, a freshly changed Hope is handed back to me.

Sitting with my knees bent, I plonk her on my tummy, facing towards me, her chubby legs dangling by my sides. When I smile her face lights up with excitement and it strikes me just how beautiful she is. I stroke the thin wisps of dark hair on her head and bop her on the nose. My reward is a big gummy smile. I pull her close to me and we snuggle and then snooze.

I wake several hours later to find myself enshrined in a thick woolen blanket. The TV hums quietly in the corner and a fire rages in the fireplace. Aunt Sophie and Brenda are cuddled up and quietly snoring in each other's arms on the other armchair and my Dad is sat beside me, straining to lip read the programme he is watching. He looks at me as I shift in my seat and yawn.

"How long have I been asleep?" I ask.

"Hours," he says, "I think you needed it. Feeling better?" he puts his arm around my shoulders and we both inspect Hope, who has her face mushed against my chest, sleeping deeply.

"I definitely did." I say yawning again. "Any chance of a cup of tea?" I ask cheekily, signaling to the baby, as if to say, "I would but...you know". Dad rolls his eyes and hefts himself off the sofa with considerable effort. I attempt to shift into a more comfortable position, my bottom having gone numb some time earlier and then reach for the TV remote control, notching the volume up slightly. The program is a fly on the wall documentary following ambulance crews as they tend to emergency calls. I watch as the paramedics and policemen approach a woman balanced on the edge of a multi storey car park. She is threatening to jump. Her boyfriend turns up out of the blue and wrestles her down, despite the protests of the emergency services. She yells and swears and paces about the car park.

Dad arrives back with two steaming mugs and gingerly hands mine to me, careful not to risk any being spilt on the sleeping Hope. We settle down to watch as the young girl is eventually handcuffed whilst weeping inconsolably and then is taken back to the police station. The narrator explains that she would be held in a police cell for her own safety, as there were insufficient grounds to have her sectioned under the mental health act, where she would receive the help and support that she required.

"Poor girl." Dad mutters. I nod.

"I'm thinking I might retrain. When Hope is a little older." I say.

"Oh yes?"

"I might train as a counsellor or a mental health nurse. I haven't quite decided which is more feasible for a working single mum." Dad considers what I have said for a while.

"I think that is a great idea and it is wonderful to hear you are thinking about the future again," I sense a but coming, "but make sure you give yourself time to recover before you rush into anything." He adds.

"I know. I will. It's going to be a while before I feel

that I can leave Hope. But when I do, I will need a new challenge to focus on, or I think my brain will turn into cabbage."

"Okay, well just as long as you don't rush into it. That said I can always help out from time to time." He adds enthusiastically.

"I can help look after the baby while you train", came a groggy voice from the other sofa. Aunt Sophie untangles herself from Brenda and sits up, trying to pat her unruly hair back down presumably in a futile bid to look like a responsible child-minding type.

"Thank you, Aunt Sophie. I would very much appreciate your help. I don't think I will start for a while though. I need time to get my head together." I look at Dad and he nods in agreement.

"No problem dear. Just let me know." She yawns, "Who's made a brew? Where's mine?"

"Where's mine?" parrots Brenda in a sleepy voice. Dad sighs.

"Fine, fine." He says hefting himself up once more.

"Oh, can you warm up a bottle for Hope while you're up?" I ask.

"Yes, but only if I can feed her?" Dad offers with far too much enthusiasm.

With the baby fed and changed, I make my way up to my bedroom. Luckily the room is large enough to accommodate all of the paraphernalia that inevitably comes with a newborn, without feeling too cluttered. I pull the moses basket onto one side of the double bed and crawl gratefully under the covers. Despite my epic nap, I am still dog-tired. Aunt Sophie and Brenda's room is next door to mine and they have chirpily offered to jump in and take care of Hope in the morning so that I can get a much-needed lie in. I could have cried tears of joy at their offer and settle for a grateful hug. I place a glass of water by the side of the bed and neck the first two of my pills, along with a herbal sleeping aid I picked up at the pharmacy. I peek over the edge of the basket, where Hope is already breathing deeply, as I do so I notice a sharp drop in temperature. My breath is coming out in white misty clouds and I shiver. The room is dark, and I sweep a look around not knowing what I am expecting to see.

I see her eyes first, white orbs in the corner of the room. Then she steps forward. I see her furious grimace as she sweeps into view. My heart is pounding fiercely in my chest as the apparition gathers strength in front of me. I try to recall the techniques my doctor had talked through with me just a few hours earlier. My mind is fuddled; deep breathing. I suck in a large breath. I close my eyes. I try to tune in with my surroundings. I feel the weight of the duvet on my feet. I run my fingers over the soft cashmere throw on top of the sheets. I feel the cold prickle at my face. When I open my eyes, she is still there, but fainter, her scowl mocking me.

I took another deep breath and raise my middle finger to the corner of the room.

"Piss off back to hell, Mary." I whisper into the dark. Her fury explodes but her form is fading until it blends in with the shadows and then to nothing. I snuggle back down into the covers, feeling warm and safe and drift to sleep.

Hope

CHAPTER TWENTY-FOUR

I wake the next morning feeling like I've slept for a hundred years. The grogginess that accompanies such a marathon sleeping session, is slightly less fun, but I snuggle down into the covers, staring at the ceiling until it starts to fade. I've deduced from the empty space beside me that Aunty Sophie snuck into my room in the wee hours to steal Hope before she could wake me. The display on my phone tells me it is eleven am. I haven't had a lay in this epic since university, but Matthew is due to arrive in half an hour, so I need to get my finger out. Taking my first bath in a month feels divine and I change into the freshly washed clothes, I can only suspect Brenda had secreted away the night before to wash and dry for me. The bosom of this family is a truly wonderful place to be, after the year I have had.

Feeling clean and happy, but utterly famished I slink downstairs to find the Christmas Eve preparations under way. Hope sits happily in her bouncy chair, which is placed in the centre of the kitchen table with my father sat protectively beside her. Brenda is frantically peeling potatoes for lunch and on seeing me enter the room, Aunt Sophie puts the finishing touches to a cup of tea and hands it to me with a bowl of porridge.

"I thought I heard the bath being run. How are you feeling love?" she says.

"About a billion times better. Thank you for taking baby duty this morning." I place the bowl and mug on the table, leaning over to give Hope a kiss. She kicks her legs excitedly causing the seat to bounce manically up and down.

"Do we know if he's bringing his floozy?" Brenda yells over her shoulder, "Just so I know for lunch."

"Err...I don't know, and I didn't want to ask. Sorry." I say watching Dad and Aunt Sophie exchange a look.

"I don't want that bloody woman here. I swear I will bitch-slap the living daylights out of her." Aunt Sophie growls and I guffaw, almost spitting out my porridge in the process.

"It's fine. Really it is." I say when I've finished my mouthful, "She is welcome to him. I'm honestly much happier without that selfish, little man-child in my life." Brenda cheers, but Dad looks dubious. The doorbell shrills and the adults in the room exchange an irritated look. He is ten minutes early. Dad marches out to meet him while I wolf down some more of my porridge, before lifting Hope out of the chair. Everyone in the kitchen listens carefully to see if they can make out a female voice. As Suzy's irritating giggle echoed down the hallway, Brenda waves the knife she has been using to slice potatoes and waves it threateningly at the door with a scowl. "Really it's fine." I say firmly.

I enter the living room to find Matthew sat fidgeting on the sofa, with Suzy sat so close she could practically be on his lap. He isn't paying any attention to her though. He looks up to me and to his daughter, nestled in my arms and his jaw drops. I realise instantly that this was the right thing to do. We had been waiting for this moment for the best part of a decade and whilst this was not how we could ever imagine it would be, it still feels good.

"Matthew, I'd like to introduce you to your daughter. This is Hope." I say. Matthew is across the room in a heartbeat to take the proffered baby from my arms.

"Christ Tess, she's beautiful." He mutters as he shifts her into the nook of his arm. Suzy stumbles across the room in her ridiculous stilettos, barging past my Dad to gate-crash in on the tender family moment.

"Aww" she squeals making the baby jump, "Isn't she adorable!" We all ignore her. Matthew turns back to the sofa and sits down barely taking his eyes off tiny Hope. As Suzy trots along behind him, I take the opportunity to check for a baby bump, but her stomach is still flat with no sign of a pregnancy. I don't find it hard to feel sympathy for her. Not only was she stuck with my knob of an ex-husband, she had lost her own baby or their trip to the baby shop in Winchester had been in anticipation of a pregnancy that just didn't happen. I make a mental note to try and have a quiet word with her later to see if she is ok. I know the pain of losing a baby. Nobody, not even someone as odious as her, deserves to go through that.

Matthew is clearly in awe of the tiny human being that he has unwittingly created with me, exploring her little hands and her nose and saying her name over and over, while Suzy crows over his shoulder, obviously desperate for a hug herself. Dad has the look of someone who had just lost a round of Nutella or Poo but is biting his tongue to keep the atmosphere from turning sour. I sink into the heavy sofa opposite them, watching Matthew fussing over his little daughter and in that moment, I am sure I see a hint of the man that I had married, many years ago. The crooked smile on his handsome face is at once entirely familiar and still oddly alien to me. So much has happened in these short months, I know without any doubt that the link between us had been irreparably severed, but from today a new one will start to form. A friendship of sorts that will give Hope two reasonably civil parents, which is all we can aim for.

Hope squirms uncomfortably in Matthew's arms, mewling in distress. Both Matthew and Suzy panic and I enjoy the scene, knowing what will occur next. A stream of milky white vomit springs out of Hope's mouth, bypassing Matthew entirely and landing with a sloppy plop on Suzy's fussy blouse. Suzy yelps and jumps up, a look of indignation on her face. Dad shows her to the downstairs bathroom, while I try to hide a wry grin under my hand.

"I can't believe she's mine." Matthew says quietly.

"Well, she's definitely yours," I reply huffily, "there hasn't been anyone-else." He fixes me with a serious Matthew stare, one eyebrow raised, but his eyes are kind for once.

"That's not what I meant. I'm just amazed. I have a daughter." I nod, I'm still trying to get my head around it myself. Something about the way he is holding her close to him tells me that I won't be getting many cuddles with my own daughter today, and that's okay. He needs to make up for lost time.

"I brought her some presents." He says nodding to a plastic carrier bag stuffed with brightly wrapped presents. "Would you mind if she opens them today?"

"She's going to struggle to open anything herself, but I'm happy for you to open them with her." I smile at him, to show I'm relaxed and comfortable with our situation. All that matters now is our daughter and there are no hard feelings with me. Our eyes meet lingeringly, as Suzy bustles noisily through the door, followed by my Dad, who looks like he wants to roll his eyes. She is explaining her current ultra-squat marathon workout plan with great enthusiasm.

Aunt Sophie appears, looking Suzy up and down with a disapproving stare.

"Would anyone like a cup of tea?" she asks stiffly.

"Oh yes please, but oh, do you have an organic decaf green tea?" Suzy asks. Sophie glowers at her not saying a word. The room falls silent as everyone looks from Sophie to Suzy, the atmosphere growing tenser and more awkward as every second passes. Eventually Suzy folds, "If not normal tea would be lovely." Aunt Sophie nods and the rest of us make our requests. Before she scuttles off back down the hallway, she fires one last sullen look at Suzy loaded with as much venom as she can muster. I hear Suzy whisper not very quietly to Matthew "I don't think she likes me." And I struggle to suppress a laugh.

Matthew stands up, Hope still snuggled in his arms, and walks round to the Christmas tree, sitting cross legged on the floor by his pile of presents. Suzy follows him eagerly, buzzing about him in a way that I suspect he finds irritating, although he is making an effort to hide it. I know him too well. Sitting Hope in his lap, her back rested against his tummy, he pulls the presents out one by one and lays them out in front of them. Hope is captivated by the shining metallic wrapping paper and gurgles with excitement, legs kicking out like she doing the River Dance. I had thought that seeing the two of them with my baby, I might feel a pang of jealousy, as though I was being left out of something important. Perhaps it was the sedatives kicking in, or the calming influence of a bit of festive spirit, but all I can feel is contentment.

The afternoon is spent in relaxed fashion, Matthew holding onto his daughter with a paternal protectiveness, I suspect that would last for the rest of his life. Suzy is largely ignored, although I feared for her safety when she criticised Brenda's cooking, surreptitiously spitting an "undercooked" carrot into a napkin with a grimace. It took several minutes for Aunt Sophie's white-knuckle grip on her knife to ease and for everyone-else to relax. By the time they are ready to leave, the sky is growing dark, and Suzy, who seems surprised to realise that she is a less than welcome guest, is sat in his car, arms crossed in a huff while Matthew and I stand at the front door saying goodbye.

"Anyway, so you're looking really well." He says with a charming smile.

"Don't."

"I mean it. You're looking really happy and relaxed. It suits you." He looks serious now and I feel a flutter of butterflies in my stomach. The car horn blasts and we both jump. Suzy is scowling at us from the car.

"Don't say anything," he says in a hushed voice, "but I'm leaving her in the New Year." I roll my eyes. "I don't suppose..." I take a big step backwards.

"Nope. Nope. A trillion times nope." We're both smiling and he holds out his arms in protest. "Merry Christmas Matthew. Goodbye" I close the door on him.

"Aww Tess..." he says as the door closes firmly in his face. I hear him chuckle, before his footsteps tap away.

Hope naps as the adults of the household jump into action, doing dishes and preparing for the festivities to come the next day. By the time we flop down on the sofa, the night sky is pitch black and the white lights of the Christmas tree twinkle decadently haloed by the darkness beyond. My Dad builds a huge fire to beat off the biting coldness. Hope is practising her lap standing, her chubby little legs bouncing up and down on my legs, mouth open wide with excitement. I pull her close to me and go to kiss her cheek. She turns at the last moment and meets my kiss with a sticky open mouth.

"Eurgh" I say and laugh.

"Oh, come now, it must be time for cuddles with Aunty Sophie." She swoops in and grasps Hope out of my hands.

My phone rings. It's Tom. I pad into the dining room, which is unfeasibly cold after the roaring warmth of the living room fire.

"Hello you." He says.

"Hey, how's it going?"

"Mischief managed. They won't be in bed for a while yet, but I spent a good two hours chasing them around the park, so shouldn't be long. Either way, they'll be out for the count soon. Just wanted to check in and see how you're doing?"

"Yeah, I'm good. All went well with Matthew today. He's completely smitten."

"Of course, he is. She's gorgeous."

"She is indeed. Listen, I need to thank you, for everything you have done for me. You really saved me."

"I didn't save you. You saved yourself. I just stood beside you and held your hand." I realise that he is right, and I feel a pride in myself I haven't felt for a long time blossoming.

"Well, either way, I can't thank you enough."

"How about that drink?" I can hear from his voice he is smiling.

"Ah, I'm not allowed to drink. How about dinner instead?" I say

"Seems reasonable." He says. "I'll pick you up at seven on Boxing day?"

"It's a date." I say, a mammoth grin on my face.

"Great. Merry Christmas Tess." He murmurs down the phone.

I flump back down on the sofa with a happy sigh. Aunt Sophie and Brenda are fussing over Hope on the other sofa and my Dad wraps his arm around my shoulder and I snuggle in. I've always loved Christmas Eve, but there is something very magical about my first Christmas with my own daughter.

"You ok?" my Dad asks planting a sloppy kiss on my forehead.

"Yep, I'm good." I say and for the first time all year, I mean it.

CHAPTER TWENTY-FIVE

Tom and I hold hands as we walk towards the church. Hope toddles along in front of us, swishing her white satin skirt around her legs and stopping occasionally to bend down and pick at the flowers that line the path.

"So, what did Matthew say?" asks Tom.

"He called it an 'extraordinary act of love'." I say with a smirk and he chuckles.

"Of course. What guy wouldn't appreciate his girlfriend arranging a surprise wedding for him?"

"Oh, I'm glad to hear that!" I say and give him a gentle shove with my arm. He doesn't let go of my hand, but he doesn't look at me either so I'm struggling to judge his reaction. I decide to leave it there. It is far too early (still) in our relationship for either of us to be considering marriage and the thought of him proposing sends a flutter of anxiety through me. It's not that I don't want to marry him; of course I do. He's handsome, kind and best of all he gets me. It's just the cruel reality of a marriage break up is still quite raw in my memory and in spite of all of the positive signs that our relationship will endure, I'm still smarting and nervous.

Eighteen months of counselling has achieved a lot. I'm not sure how the simple act of sitting with a stranger and spilling out every crazy and anxious thought that comes into my head, is actually helping me. But somehow, I feel improved and renewed. I've fixed parts of myself that I didn't even realise were broken. I'm more aware of myself, the reasons why I am the way I am. I am fragile but brave, but most of all I am ok. Finally.

The path turns around to the right, and the church entrance comes into sight. Two ushers guard the doors handing out the orders of service. Everyone is solemn faced. This is a curious gathering to be sure. We walk out of the heat of the warm spring day into the cool dark church and take our seats on the left-hand side. I spot Matthew stood pale faced at the front of the church chewing furiously on a nail.

"Look." I say to Tom and he follows my gaze.

"Christ, he looks like a condemned man."

"Bless. I think he would have done anything he could to try and wriggle out of this." I whisper, not wanting to be overheard by the other guests in case they think I just have a massive case of sour grapes, "But she'd already booked everything, church, reception venue, even the flights to ship his granny over from Cork. He'd never willingly lose that much money."

There's a sudden kerfuffle from the back of the church and it becomes apparent that the bride has arrived. Matthew blanches and looks like he is actually going to vomit. Tom and I try to suppress our giggles. Everyone in the church stands and I help Hope stand on the seat next to us, so that she can see her Daddy and Suzy tie the knot. I'd felt a bit put out that Suzy hadn't wanted Matthew's only daughter to be a bridesmaid at their wedding, but she was appalled at the prospect of being upstaged by an unruly toddler. Thankfully, Hope is too young to know any better, but I'm sure one day Matthew will have some explaining to do.

Suzy appears at the back of the church, resplendent in a full skirted, sparking, princess-style wedding gown, clutching onto the arm of a weary looking old man who I presume is her father. Although frail and bent, he wore an expression of sheer determination, as if no physical pains could prevent him from reaching the end of the aisle and depositing his high-maintenance daughter to become someone-else's responsibility. Surprisingly, Matthew is no longer looking quite so panic stricken. His mouth hangs open as he watches his bride swish up the church aisle. I can see it in him, I've always known him better than he knew himself, this is right for him and he is going to be happy.

There would have been a time that realization would

have left me reeling with dismay; why wasn't I good enough? Now though, I can see we just weren't right for one another and that's ok. It doesn't mean I'm any less of a person than Suzy. It's not a competition after all. Although if it were, I reckon I might be winning. My man is miles better than hers.

The End

Thank you for reading my novel.
Receiving reviews on platforms such as Amazon and Goodreads is crucial for all authors, particularly self-published authors like myself.

At the time of writing this I have 4 reviews on Amazon, all 5 star rated, which rather gives the impression they were all written by my Mum (they weren't - she only gave it 1 star and refused to leave a review on Amazon).

It would mean a huge amount to me if you would be willing to leave a review of this book, whether good, bad or indifferent on any online platform. I would be hugely grateful.

Thank you!

Hope

ABOUT THE AUTHOR

Sarah Branch lives with her husband, in a little lodge house in the heart of the Hampshire countryside. Her current inventory boasts 2 children, 2 step-children, 2 cats (1 of which is psychotic), 2 ferrets and 5 chickens. Life is very busy, but she still finds time to read and write.

This is Sarah's first novel.

Her second novel, Tracey Cringle hasn't got a clue is available on Amazon.

Printed in Great Britain
by Amazon